The Funeral of the Living
And
The Wedding of the Dead

Written by

Shi Yi

Copyright © 2024 by Shi Yi

To the people I love.

Table of Contents

Preface

I have never felt inclined to call myself a writer; I usually refer to myself as "the author of this text," or, more formally, "the copyright holder." If readers happens to read what I have written, I hope that after finishing my work, they might say, with a sense of lingering satisfaction, "Well-written," and then simply refer to me as "that person who writes."

I attribute this desire to my understanding of life. To be specific, no matter where you are in the world, ugly things always present themselves with brazen openness, while beautiful things tend to hide in shyness. This understanding has shaped my criteria for evaluating any literary work: a "great" work is never imagined; it is a distillation of reality—a thorough and objective record of what people see and think, allowing readers to sift through it for what they need, inspiring their thoughts and reflections, and ultimately influencing their very selves.

Thus, the author is not a creator of plots but a narrator of reality. Such writing often feels dark because reality itself is dark, but to me, the task of the writer is never to please the readers; it is to resonate with them. The word "resonance" is neutral—it can evoke feelings of oppression and fear, or calm and joy. Moreover, "resonance" varies from person to person. Even when faced with the same passage, due to each individual's different life circumstances, emotional needs, and areas of focus, the reactions are never the same. Therefore, the author needs to maintain a relatively neutral stance, to see themselves as a storyteller who unearths the essence of the story, leaving the space for thought to the readers, rather than merely venting emotions for self-gratification.

I have always been interested in exploring many themes: life and death, love and hate, emotion and reason, illusion and reality, desire and morality, humanity and law, war and peace, loyalty and betrayal, elegance and kitsch, meetings and farewells... The reason these seemingly opposing realities coexist is that they are not simply black and white in their moral implications; they just happen to exist side by side. As for why and how they coexist, that is a topic worthy of in-depth exploration. I believe that understanding, or even comprehending, the reasons behind this coexistence can reveal the spiritual world of a nation or even the operational principles of a country.

With these thoughts in mind, this book was born. In it, I attempt to tell a very simple story: A high school student, in a moment of casual rebellion, took a few photos of a leaking school building and posted them online, mocking the principal and venting dissatisfaction with the

school. However, this act incited a frenzy of
retaliation. Displeased with the student's disrespect,
the principal, accompanied by his best subordinates
whom the principal called "brothers" and his older
brother, visited the student's home and pushed him
down the building, causing his death. During this
period, the principal's mistress and the school's
teachers discovered valuable paintings and treasures
in the student's home and seized them. Ultimately,
to avoid a public scandal and to cover up corruption
in the school's construction process, the police
falsely declared the student's death a suicide,
hunted down students spreading negative
information about the school, and silenced the
parents until "all is well" and the dust settles.

I have divided this book into four parts: "The
Ripple," "The Ivory Pendant in the Painting,"
"Breaking Free," and "A Red Balloon." The first
part mainly describes the student's subconscious
thoughts as he lay on the operating table near death.
The second part is the principal's recollections. The
third part depicts how the art teacher underwent a
transformation in personality and behavior. The
fourth part is narrated from the perspective of the
investigating police officer. The titles of the four
chapters relate to the themes I wish to express: "The
Ripple" is like human life—from an individual
perspective, every person has a journey filled with
tumult, but from a broader perspective, it is like an

insignificant ripple, even if it involves matters of life and death. "The Ivory Pendant in the Painting" is a metaphor for the principal's actions—people kill an elephant solely for its ivory, which ultimately becomes a meaningless pendant; when the pendant is just an ornament in a painting, its significance seems even smaller. "Breaking Free" symbolizes the art teacher's transformation—she starts as a timid young teacher, goes through a series of events, and finally emerges in her "perfect" form, breaking free from the limits of morality. The police officer in the last part is like a balloon—fragile and easily broken. Yet, when he is endowed with "red," he becomes a hero in people's eyes, seemingly possessing an indestructible power—but regardless, he remains that balloon, moving cautiously to survive.

Then, when all the details and trivialities blend together, an insignificant yet extraordinary journey begins.

The Ripple

I

I could no longer recall when my nightmares had first begun. As I traced my memories backward, I always found myself feeling disoriented at certain points. At those moments, the storylines replaying in my mind vanished, only to be replaced by seemingly random people and things that leapt out from the periphery, startling me. Whenever this happened, I began to recall if there had ever been a time I had left home without shoes or if I had once spilled water onto someone's clothes by accident, until I asked myself—who was I, really?

My memories slowly unfolded, forming a vivid and lifelike scene: I was struggling against a torrent, moving upstream with nothing but my small boat; it swayed madly in the rushing current, while a group of cattle and sheep leisurely grazed on the shore, heads bowed. And there was another "me"— sitting under the shade of a lush, umbrella-like tree. My girlfriend's head rested quietly on this other "me's" lap, and "he" gently stroked her hair, watching her as she fell into a deep sleep. The slowly moving sunlight found a perfect angle, first passing through the gaps in the leaves, then through her closed eyelids, silently awakening her.

It was an abrupt tree, as if it had suddenly appeared, strikingly out of place on the flat grassland. I, still battling the noisy waters, felt disturbed by the sound, my rhythm broken. From under the shade of the tree, my girlfriend said it was not noise, but music—though heavy and overbearing, only music could attach vivid colors to the skin of life, only music could make meaningless words and phrases fade away, and only music could momentarily blur the boundaries between resentment and love.

I sat at the bow, paddling with my flimsy oar, shouting toward her, "So, what should I do now?"

But she did not seem to be speaking to me; her eyes were filled only with the other "me." That "me" sat in silence, listening to her chatter while gazing at the distant cattle and sheep. My girlfriend lazily talked about Beethoven's music and shyly flaunted the latest pop songs she had learned. The cows flicked their tails, swatting away flies, while an old sheepdog trotted along, sometimes standing, sometimes lying down, and diligently rounding up the flock to keep the mischievous lambs from wandering too far. The small temple on the hillside remained silent, the only sound being the flutter of paper money affixed to the Buddha statues. I saw the other "me" glance at my girlfriend, stroke her long black hair, and use his fingers to draw lightly in the dirt, playing a small prank on the ants crawling there, watching them scurry about in a panic, searching for their way home.

My girlfriend said, "Look at you, you can't just

keep your hands still."

That other "me" chuckled, wiping his muddy fingers on his jeans, leaving a dirt streak across them.

I considered greeting my girlfriend, but on second thought, I decided against it—shouting there would make me seem like a madman. Neither I, my girlfriend, the cattle and sheep, nor the sheepdog would probably pay me any mind, or even glance my way.

Yet, the dog suddenly raised its head, though it wasn't looking in my direction. I mustered all my strength, pushing my boat forward just a little—it was a short distance; I could still see the other "me" and my girlfriend. She had taken off her blue and white jacket, and that "me" gently placed it over her. Although her drowsiness had been dispelled by the sunlight, she still lay beside him, her head resting on his lap. I saw his hand under the jacket, stroking her belly. She suddenly shivered for half a second. She laughed, saying, "That tickles! Stop it!"

It seemed my boat had moved another centimeter—or perhaps a meter. This small progress melted away much of my fatigue. The water at my feet did not drown out the sound of the other "me" and my girlfriend speaking; perhaps it was because I had been listening closely, or maybe the turbulent current had not been as fierce as it had seemed— perhaps not even as deafening as the whispers of the grass on the riverbank. I looked down to observe the stream—clear to the bottom yet unfathomably deep. Fear began to creep over me, as I was afraid that the stream would swallow me whole. I told myself to keep my head up, and I paddled with even more force.

The sheepdog's gaze seemed never to leave the distance; it appeared only the dandelions landing on and taking off from its body understood that time was still passing. Alone, it froze time in its presence. Curious, I followed its gaze. A group of teenagers in matching blue and white jackets was walking toward the other "me" and my girlfriend. My brain commanded me to continue forward, filtering out all the surrounding noise. When my mind quieted down, I suddenly remembered—our school uniforms were exactly like that. I told myself, "Yes, those are our school uniforms. These people must be my classmates." I focused intently on what they were about to do. A chubby boy looked at the other "me" from afar, quickened his pace, and walked toward the other "me" and my girlfriend.

"It's time to gather and go home. The teachers and everyone are waiting."

"Okay."

That other "me" gently patted my girlfriend. Almost simultaneously, she used her left hand to push herself up and slowly stood, patting the dirt and grass off her clothes. The sun shone on the falling dust, its twinkling light like gold dust scattering around. In that instant, I seemed to hear a shout coming from far away:

"Ask yourself, is this a scene you have lived through?"

I could not discern whose voice it was—perhaps it had been my own inner monologue, or maybe it had been the random sound of crashing waves that just happened to form this question. I murmured, "It seems so, but back then there was no struggle against the current, no water splashing in my face." The arrhythmic clamor sometimes made me restless, sometimes helped me block out all distractions, allowing me to listen closely to the beat of my own heart, momentarily merging body and soul.

Almost as if guided by some unknown force, I wedged my small boat between the abrupt rocks in the stream, allowing myself to gaze at the distant "me." The male classmate, seeing the other "me" and my girlfriend standing up, swiftly turned around, stepping across the green grass, whispering with a mischievous smile to the others beside him. Soon, the whole group—including the other "me" and my girlfriend—caught the eye of a middle-aged man who signaled them with his gaze. All their steps cruelly trampled the tender green grass, heedlessly squeezing out every bit of moisture from each blade. Grasshoppers hiding in the grass jumped out in fear and fury, futilely attempting to protest against these humans, yet a casual step from them could turn the grasshoppers into wandering ghosts.

I could not bear to keep watching, so I resumed my struggle against the stream. Who was that middle-aged man? This question suddenly brought forth a strange thought: a name was a prison whose theoretical purpose was only to imprison a kind of inmate called "humans." The definition of "humans" might just be a combination of body and soul. Some people even believed that names could predict or control the future of these prisoners who were confined and even tormented. Was this reasonable? No, it was not. I convinced myself that it did not matter if I could not recall this man's name; his title, reputation, and wealth were worthless. I only needed to copy his image.

He was a tall, thin man, seemingly in his fifties, the only one in the group without glasses. His fingers seemed exceptionally active—at one moment, pointing into the distance, causing some students in black backpacks and school uniforms to move mechanically in that direction; at another moment, he tapped on a nearby bus, and the remaining students lined up and boarded it, one by one. Through the bus driver's window, I saw another dark-skinned man. He rested his bare feet

on the oversized steering wheel, holding a cigarette
between his index and middle fingers. He took a
deep drag and blew the smoke outside.

He must have been the driver. The bus turned
and headed into the distance, and I unhesitatingly
planned my next route in my mind. I dreaded
finding myself disoriented again the next time I
stopped. I wished for a mast to suddenly rise from
my little boat so I could climb up and hopefully find
a pier that could connect all my footsteps into a
complete line. But no pier magically appeared. I
could only note the position of that large tree and
silently prayed that it remembered what had
happened beneath it.

I continued rowing my boat. The current
suddenly grew stronger, forcefully pushing me back
toward where I had come from. I did not wish to
remain trapped in past memories—I had to strive
forward. My mind thought this, and my hands and
feet exerted more force. After chasing for a long
time, exhausted, I finally saw that I had arrived at a
brightly lit city, where the other "me" and my
girlfriend were getting off the bus together. I looked
up at the sky and the surroundings; the objects
around me slowly coalesced, then transformed into
a sculptor's chisel, etching a line on my brain's
frontal lobe:

"Spring, grasslands, school outing, my
girlfriend and me."

This chisel had a texture—the handle was ice-cold, but the tip had warmed with my body heat. I could not tell whether to describe this sharp tool as gentle or cruel; at times, it thrust me into the endless cold winds of the South Pole, at other times, it pulled me back into the Sahara at noon. I awkwardly smiled and said to the chisel:

"You, chisel, only know to obey the orders of the handle. What else can you do besides that?"

As expected, neither the chisel's tip nor handle answered my question. Instead, a reflected beam of light flashed in my eyes, so I closed my mouth and ignored that hunk of metal.

The sun hurried off duty, making way for the moon to take its place. When I was finally able to make out the faces of the other "me" and my girlfriend, I noticed that both of us had our hands in our thin pockets. I laughed and called out to the distant "me":

"Take your hands out and hold hers."

No sooner had I spoken than I regretted it. I was merely a ghost outside of time; how could I interfere in the trivialities of the human world? My supposedly deafening shout might have been no more piercing to others than the sudden chirp of a bird. I decided to sit at the bow, watching "me" and my girlfriend walk together. Suddenly, that other "me" said, "I am a bit hungry."

A sparkle lit up in my girlfriend's eyes—a

gleam that shot straight into the sky, even though
the laughter that followed squinted her eyes into
slits. The love in the other "me's" eyes sprang forth,
gathering irresistibly around her. Watching from
afar, I felt a twinge of jealousy. My girlfriend took
two one-yuan[1] coins out of her pocket, tossing them
playfully in her hand, the sound of metal colliding.
She handed me one of the coins with a smile and
said, "Let's get two sesame buns. I want a sweet
one. You want one with meat, right?"

As she spoke, she pointed to a bun stand in the
distance. My thoughts told me that spring had not
only come for the grass and that big tree, but also
for animals like us, whom we temporarily called
"human." Who could witness this tender scene
without feeling moved? Be it officials or merchants,
common folk or nobility—when spring arrived, it
turned the order of the human world upside down.
As I faced the spring hues under the night, a sense
of loss and bitterness welled up within me. The
streetlights in the city shone with a pale yellow
light, stealing the moon's stage. Their glow pulled
the steam from the bun stand upward in erratic
spirals.

That other "me" handed the two coins to the
elderly bun vendor. The old woman bent over, tore
two buns from the inside wall of an oil barrel, and
wrapped them in a thin white plastic bag. As soon
as they were wrapped, the bag filled instantly with

white steam. With just one bite, that other "me" devoured half a bun. My girlfriend tore off half of her bun and asked "me" if I wanted to try the sweet one. "I" agreed.

I, too, felt hungry, yet had no idea how to satiate it—night never provided people with food, nor did it care for their survival. I thought spring was the same; it offered only a bit of ridiculous pleasure, utterly ignorant of the suffering that lay everywhere. It moved through barren alleys, kissed passionate hotels, slipped into royal chambers, but only shrugged and told me that it had no right to upset the order of the universe, only to begin work on time.

I sighed. This cruel season said nothing but brushed past my eyes with a gust of wind, letting me see more clearly. I chastised myself, the other me, and my girlfriend, "How… how could you smile?"

The chisel reappeared out of nowhere, its handle patting my thigh, forcibly dragging my gaze away and moving it next to my forehead. This time, I examined the metallic object closely—it was smooth enough to reflect a silhouette, but not my own. I stared at it, and it carved a second line:

"Question: How can you smile?"

I mocked it for its lack of grammar, but it seemed incapable of speaking or perhaps simply too disdainful to respond. Having finished carving, it turned to leave. I waved at it, mimicking Xu Zhimo on the Cambridge Bridge, but it vanished abruptly, leaving me unable to catch even a glimpse of its back.

I steered my little boat onward. The waters ahead began to calm, and the sun unexpectedly jumped back up from the other side. I thought, "Let's take a break," and laid the oars across the bow, slowly sitting down to look around at the scenery, trying to recall what details I had missed along the way. I could not remember; if I could, perhaps I could calculate how much longer until I reached the end. I seemed to accept this fact—that one self should be an observer while another self remains immersed in the performance being watched; it seemed more interesting than participating myself.

"Come home."

My mother's voice came from behind. Instinctively, I turned to look for her figure but saw nothing. I scanned my surroundings and finally saw her in front of the boat. She was standing at the school gate, holding a leather bag bought from a street stall ten years ago, ignoring the bustling students passing by, her eyes fixed on the school gate until the other "me" appeared in her line of sight. A misty fog billowed from the nearby steamed bun shop, accompanied by the strange smell of burning coal, the chatter of voices, and the unrestrained honking of car horns. I felt my eyes, nostrils, and ears were all being occupied, even though I was only watching the performance of the other "me."

I stared fixedly as the other "me" and my mother met at the school gate and began walking down the road. I instinctively stayed on the boat because there was always a voice telling me to wait. I asked, "Wait for what?" There was no response. I shouted again, "Wait for what?" Still, there was no answer. "Then just wait," I thought.

Waiting is always long and tedious, and in my waiting, there was a trace of uneasiness. I did not know what I was waiting for—perhaps a new bicycle that had once appeared in a dream, or maybe the flower petals that frequently fell from the street trees. I saw my girlfriend walking alone, wearing an ill-fitting school uniform and carrying a heavy black backpack, heading in a different direction. As she passed by a wall, a bird's call from the trees seemed to catch her attention, and she glanced up before continuing forward with her head down.

I muttered to myself, "These two trees look so familiar." They grew symmetrically on either side of the wall, each reaching out a branch toward the other, ultimately entangling elegantly. Then I remembered. I once said goodbye to my girlfriend under these trees on a sweltering summer day, enjoying a moment of coolness while lightly brushing her hand with the back of mine. I liked these unscheduled farewells—I feared calculating the time and manner of saying goodbye alone, for it not only felt lonely but often meant that I would never see the person I was bidding farewell to again or that when we met again, we would be like strangers. Every time this happened, I would ask myself: if separation is inevitable, why meet at all? I was sure I did not like it; it was better to be like these two trees, perhaps never able to embrace each other, but always able to meet, even if their branches and leaves continually grew, fell, and finally returned to the earth.

The stream that battled with me flowed through the city, where the riverbed was no longer filled with massive natural rocks but replaced by concrete. The water washed away every footprint in front of me, making them unrecognizable, yet it brought me to my girlfriend's doorstep. I watched as she entered her home, switched on the incandescent light in the kitchen, and skillfully took rice from the sack, rinsed it, and finally put it in the rice cooker, absentmindedly pressing the cook button. She then walked into the bedroom, turned on only the desk lamp, and drew the curtains. Her slender silhouette soon appeared on the curtains; it seemed she had changed into her home clothes. I realized I had forgotten once again that she could not hear my voice, so I shouted from downstairs:

"Eat more!"

I comforted myself, thinking, if she cannot hear, so be it. Maybe she can feel it. I heard her, during the time the rice was cooking, open the piano, flip through the sheet music, and begin to play a tune I did not understand. Her music could seamlessly connect pain and joy; at that moment, she no longer seemed like the dusty, hunched-over high school girl, but a woman isolated from the world. The music liberated her hands and her soul. This music might have been casually written by the composer, but in her hands, it became her weapon—she was attacking the vulgar and coarse world that encircled her, even though tomorrow, she would once again fall into the familiar world we know—the world that issues passes to the despicable and forces everyone to wear masks.

I truly wanted to stay and listen to every note flowing from her fingertips. The rice cooker's button popped up, signaling the end of everything. Suddenly, I remembered why I was in this stream— to pursue my memories, find each node, and connect them into a line. So, I gripped the oars and continued paddling forward.

The sunlight caught up with me once more. The spring scenery remained unchanged, becoming a sacred, inviolable backdrop for this journey of mine. I scolded myself for always trying to find fault with spring in this season of revival. As I guided my boat upstream to climb higher, I justified myself, saying that I could not change anything anyway, so I might as well complain freely. In the distance, the bell of the Catholic Church rang, sounding as if it agreed with my thoughts.

I reached a shallow bank and deliberately beached the boat so I could gaze upon this city before me. What is the name of this city? I had forgotten. Just like people's names, the name of a city has no meaning; the only meaningful thing is the memory associated with it. At that moment, I was a person who had lost his memory. Those occasional fragmented memories that popped up were no longer enough to piece together everything about myself. I could only keep moving forward, searching for clues from the past. Then, the other "me" appeared in my sight just in time—it turned out the stream had led me to the home of that "me." Suddenly, I no longer harbored any grudges against the stream for blocking my way earlier. The water slapped against the stones on the shore and whispered to me:

"See for yourself. And look carefully."

That other "me" walked with urgent steps to the front door. As the heavy door was opened by that other "me," the whole city was instantly filled with noise. The noise came from the living room, the bedroom, the kitchen of that "me's" house... I could not make out anyone's conversation, not even a single word. I blamed the sound of the stream for being too noisy and ordered it to shut up. It quieted down, but I still could not make out what information was contained in the noise inside the house. The stream, seeing this, resumed its former turbulence; to me, it seemed to be mocking my incompetence with all its might or loudly proclaiming its innocence.

I shouted loudly, hoping to draw the attention of anything around, but my eyes and ears never left that house. At first, the distant house grew larger before my eyes, gradually moving closer until it was within arm's reach, eventually looming arrogantly right in the middle of the stream. My little boat crept forward slowly. When my hand touched the red brick wall, I heard every brick's conversation: they were complaining about the gray cement forcibly clinging to their bodies, discussing the delicacies they had tasted yesterday, envying a plush shark toy that could sleep in bed every day, explaining the principles of thunderstorms and hail, showing off their collection of knives, mocking the casual artwork created on the windowsill, savoring the petals of the luxurious hawthorn flowers, and enjoying the thrill as electricity surged through them.

"Nothing means anything; when the world is full of meaningless things, your world will have meaning."

The calm water said this to me. I despised its rambling and could not empathize with its chaotic logic. I ignored its teachings and just watched the lively bricks continue their revelry. When they finally calmed down a bit, the stream slapped my left cheek heavily. That reminded me—so I walked to the bow, teetered on my tiptoes, and tried to peek through the window to see what drama might be playing out in that dimly lit room.

My hand lightly touched the rough cement of the windowsill, then slowly shifted my weight onto it. Perhaps my abrupt behavior had defiled the windowsill, for it commanded the glass to open its gaping maw and lunge at me, forcing me to fall back into the boat. The splash of water interrupted the gathering on the brick wall; each red brick stared at me in astonishment before turning to look at the sky, shouting in unison:

"It's coming, it's coming!"

So I looked up with them. A woman, her face concealed, stood upon the dark clouds, drawing colorful objects from her bag and hurling them down with a firm, powerful stance. The things she tossed fell heavily into the water, then floated up, gradually gathering around me and my boat. Only then did I see clearly what these things were—they were opened bags of cement, fragrant snacks, a shark plush toy with strands of her hair still clinging to it, a blood-stained knife, inexplicable ink paintings, scattered hawthorn blossoms, and bundles of frayed wires. I picked one item from each type, carefully placing it at the back of the boat for safekeeping, thinking perhaps these were my passes for the next stop. Then I looked up and said to the brick wall:

"Oh, these are the things you were talking about."

The bricks burst into laughter, clearly mocking me. I wondered in my heart what was so laughable about me, but I could not come up with an answer.

II

"People are always eager to draw a fine red line to keep disaster isolated from their world, not realizing that when the red line breaks, it will do so without a sound. Disaster will silently sever that line, and then, without hesitation, invade the other side. By the time people notice the arrival of disaster, much of their life has already been devoured, and they can only helplessly wail at their fragmented bodies and souls."

I had told myself this long ago, not just warning myself in words but writing it down, engraving those words and punctuation marks into my memory. When these words echoed around me once more, the house in front of the stream suddenly collapsed, yet it did not stir a single ripple in the water. Instead, a stiff curtain took its place. I knew I had to move forward, so with a nervous heart, I went to the stern to retrieve the knife I had picked up earlier, intending to cut through the curtain. But my little boat calmly passed right through it. Ahead, there seemed to be no difference from the scene I encountered before—I was once again pushed by the current to the foot of my girlfriend's building. I asked the stream why it had brought me back, and it responded by enthusiastically splashing against the stones on the bank while answering in a calm tone:

"Since you have come, you might as well stay."

I was about to scold it for wasting my time but immediately held back. I realized that while this was a place I had been before, the time was certainly different—it was now broad daylight, presumably midday. So, I kept my eyes fixed intently on my girlfriend's house, scanning for any details that might have been missed. Soon, heavy and hurried footsteps echoed from the hallway of her building. I could tell it was the angry pounding of sneakers on concrete stairs, the resonance of a heart pounding out of rhythm and transmitting its chaos downward.

She appeared downstairs. Beads of sweat on her forehead encased the glaring sunlight, sending it exploding into my eyes. I rubbed my eyes, straining to see what she would do. She was running so fast that I froze in place; in no time, she ran out of my sight. I hurriedly grabbed the oars and used all my strength to chase after her in the direction she had left. When she finally became exhausted, I found myself, in a daze, once again in front of the house of that other "me."

"You've met again," I said, standing on the boat in a bad mood. Yet, I quickly realized I should have referred to the other "me" and my girlfriend as "we," not "you." My curiosity suppressed the urge to correct myself, and I decided to keep watching.

The other "me" appeared as well—he walked up to my girlfriend, gently stroked the corner of her eye with his thumb. My girlfriend slowly bent down, adjusted the position of her legs, and gradually knelt on the hard, scorching concrete ground. From out of nowhere, she conjured a yellow cloth strip and tightly gripped it in her hand, while the other "me" lay down calmly, indifferent to the temperature of the pavement, allowing her to kneel beside him in this strange posture. Seeing him lying down, she slowly opened her hand and released the captive yellow strip, then slowly spread her arms and embraced the "me" lying on the ground, falling asleep together.

Their movements were so slow, so unhurried, that it unearthed a sense of drowsiness in me. I diverted my gaze—I saw that the once noisy brick wall had lost its vitality, becoming lifeless; the window that had once opened its gaping maw to chase me had already been defeated. Its mouth remained wide open, showing no sign of movement, and its terrifying fangs had been completely removed, leaving only a shattered upper and lower jaw.

I attempted to climb up to the edge of the windowsill once more, smashing the once-devouring maw with a single punch. This gave me unprecedented confidence—I leapt lightly into the room, only to find it filled with people, and the other "me" was there too. I could not help but ask him:

"Are not you downstairs?"

Of course, the other "me" did not answer— time seemed nonexistent here, and everything, people and objects alike, was utterly still. So, I boldly moved through the crowd and immediately spotted a familiar face. I tried to recall everyone I had encountered from the beginning, but I could not remember who he was. The stream mocked me, saying:

"Names do not matter. You said so yourself."

I was not angry at its taunting; on the contrary, I was grateful for the reminder—the familiar face had once appeared by the rushing waters, with a bus behind him, and in front of the bus, there was a patch of grass with a solitary tree growing on it. He was pointing at the other "me" with his right index finger while holding a stack of printed papers with his remaining fingers, and droplets of saliva were frozen midair, spraying from his mouth. I cautiously wove through this barrage of saliva and found my father and mother on the other side of the crowd. Four men wearing glasses were each gripping my father and mother's arms, seemingly trying to make them sit on a sofa, while my father appeared to be trying to stand up. The two men beside my father must have been exerting considerable force—the veins in their hands were bulging, and their visible arm hair stood upright.

I returned to the crowd, wanting to take a closer look at everyone. I noticed there was a woman among them—and only one woman. She impressed me because she bore an uncanny resemblance to my girlfriend, only older. Though the wrinkles at the corners of her eyes suggested she might be around forty, age had not ravaged her figure. She wore a tight pencil skirt and high heels, with a rolled-up canvas under her left arm, likely a painting; her right hand held a large parcel. Her long black hair looked smooth and flowing, contrasting sharply with my mother's dry, yellowed strands. But I suddenly realized she seemed to be facing the opposite direction from the crowd—she was heading toward the door, looking as if she was in a hurry to leave. No one tried to stop her.

Though everything was frozen in time, the scene before me sent chills down my spine. It meant this was no ordinary day; something significant must have happened. My curiosity, mixed with a sense of urgency, sent my heart racing uncontrollably, pounding wildly in my chest. This feeling was both real and surreal—my heart beat rhythmically against every inch of my skin, yet I had no memory of this sensation, as if it had never occurred before.

The stream waited patiently for me, not moving an inch. At that moment, I wished it would make some random noise to rescue me from this deathly silence, but it did not care about my thoughts. I walked to the windowsill where the gaping maw had once been and climbed out with both hands and feet. The stream still ignored me, merely sending up a cluster of lotus pods from beneath the water—there were no green leaves or bright flowers, only bare pods on each stalk. They shot up from the water, first straight up into the sky, then all bowed their heads in unison, directing their faces toward me, surrounding me completely. As I stood there in bewilderment, all the lotus pods suddenly emitted a yellow light through each hole. The brightness made me forget whether it was noon or midnight; I only knew I had to close my eyes, using my eyelids to filter out some of the blinding light.

After I closed my eyes, it felt as though I had slept. My eyelids, already heavy, closed easily but were hard to open. Only when I heard a piano melody did I muster the courage to open them—the tune seemed familiar; it must have been the one my girlfriend was playing in the distance. Accompanied by the music, she murmured to herself:

"I want to be drunk with you in an ocean of whiskey."

I turned towards the sound, only to see a barren wasteland; fortunately, those hideous lotus pods were gone. I laughed, thinking that my girlfriend had probably never tasted a drop of whiskey, and all the flavors were the product of her baseless imagination. I told myself that, perhaps for her, only an unattainable future would taste like whiskey—rich and romantic.

After she finished speaking, she fell silent, but I faintly smelled the scent of alcohol—I realized that my sense of smell hadn't been lost. Was this the smell of whiskey? I did not know; it was sharp, like the cheap spirits drunk by old alcoholics or the disinfectant alcohol used in hospitals. I suspected that the alcohol was a clue, so I decided to follow the scent to its source, only to find that the alcohol had already permeated every bit of air around me. At this moment, I wished I were a hunting dog that could simply follow the scent.

The neighborhood before me was slowly swallowed by the endless wasteland in the distance, and the buildings of reinforced concrete were no match for it; only this house still stood. I thought, the clue must be here, so I should go inside again. I patted my little boat and said to it:

"Wait for me."

This time, the stream was not as deathly still as before; it occasionally rippled, gently lapping at everything along the shore. I chose not to climb in through the window this time—perhaps that was why I had missed something before. This time, I decided to enter through the front door, like a normal person. As I approached the door, I hesitated: What would I see this time? Could I open this door successfully? Would I be able to get out once I entered? But this hesitation and fear were quickly devoured by curiosity and a sense of purpose. The moment I touched the doorknob, the bricks hidden beneath the wall plaster became active again: they shook off their ugly, rough paint and immediately burst into laughter.

"Go on in. Time has returned."

Time had indeed returned, and I could once again feel the turbulent sound waves inside the house. Afraid of missing any scene, I gritted my teeth and gripped the doorknob. The handle transformed into a vine that crept over every cell in my body and then dissolved me. I was terrified and asked:

"What are you doing?"

"You are everywhere."

The door did not open, yet I passed through the skin and bones of the concrete and steel, then spread evenly throughout every corner of the house. Instantly, I gained a new ability—I could feel every vibration in the house, detect every scent floating in the air, and scan every subtle expression on the faces of the people inside. My body was suspended from the ceiling, crouching on the floor, clinging to the walls, like an audience waiting for the opera to begin, sitting properly in formal attire.

I waited a long time before the "actors" began to appear, one after another. I dared not speak or gesture wildly to express my urgency, for fear of disturbing my own curiosity and being expelled. As everything around me began to stir, that man appeared again, but not alone—besides the other "me," my father, and my mother, there seemed to be a crowd of diverse people following him: the only woman, the only bald man, the only fat man, the only man in black, the only man with a flushed face, and the familiar man—the only one without glasses.

This man seemed to be the leader. He threw a stack of papers on the coffee table, his left hand in his pocket, and pointed with his right index finger at my parents, telling them to look for themselves. Only then did I have the chance to read the documents I had not managed to browse last time. The man thoughtfully spread each page on the redwood coffee table in the living room, pointing to the first page and shouting at my father:

"Look at what your son has done!"

I shifted my gaze to the top of the page. It was a few black-and-white photos printed with a low-resolution printer. The image quality was poor, but I could still make out the content: it seemed to be a scene of ruins, with thick concrete beams covered in cracks and dangling with precarious water droplets. The columns supporting the beams were also slightly cracked, and the thick paint on the walls could not hide these marks. My father said nothing, while my mother asked in confusion what had happened, and the other "me" stared directly at the man, his eyes like torches. The other "me" countered, asking if it was not true. The man did not answer but pointed to the second page.

The chisel appeared again. It showed no reaction to my presence, went straight to the wall, and engraved the number "10." Then the blade, along with the handle, moved to the top of the first page of paper and carved a big cross on it. The man seemed unaware that the first page had been damaged; he dismissively slid the second page toward my parents. As my parents' eyes scanned every detail on the paper, the man tapped his fingernail on the paper on the table, finally stopping at one line:

"The provincial key high school[2] is about to be ruined by this principal."

The other "me" and my parents seemed unsure how to respond to the man, and the people behind him showed no reaction, as if both sides were waiting for the other to break the silence. The man with the flushed face paced back and forth in boredom, occasionally glancing at the other "me" with contempt. Then he walked to the cabinet, casually picked up an unopened bottle of liquor. He grasped the bottle, twisted off the cap with a grimace, held it under his nose to sniff, and then tilted his head back to pour the liquid into his mouth. I could clearly see his throat move up and down three times as he swallowed the liquor, finally releasing the excess alcohol vapor into the air with his breath. The other "me" and my parents stared at him, stunned, until the other "me," after a long daze, shouted at the flushed-faced man:

"What are you doing?"

The shout of the other "me" was deafening. The chisel had not yet left but returned to the wall as soon as the words fell, wiping off the previously engraved "10" and engraving a "9" in the same spot. This time, it seemed quite satisfied with its work, so it called for the lotus pods I had encountered before, instructing them to light up the entire room. They surrounded the "9," examining it carefully. Seeing that I was not interested in their conversation, the lotus pods dispersed, flickering their familiar light in my eyes, trying in vain to capture my attention.

I still ignored them, as if I had an innate aversion to them.

The clamor of the crowd paused after the other "me" shouted, only to resume with the sound of breaking glass. The flushed-faced man smashed the bottle onto the floor, and the liquor splashed into every corner of the room and onto every one of my cells. Seeing this, the bald man reached out to hold the flushed-faced man back, gently patting his

chest. This soothing gesture was quite effective—
the flushed-faced man took a step back, his
clenched fists returning to his pockets.

The other "me" began to flush as well; if not
for the distinct differences in appearance between
him and the flushed-faced man, I might not have
been able to tell them apart. The man pulled out the
third page, titled "Appraisal Report," and it bore an
official seal. This page contained no lengthy
passages, just a short sentence. I intended to lean in
for a closer look, but my mother beat me to it. Her
right hand held the paper, frowning as she read. Her
trembling body resonated with the floating paper,
creating a rustling sound.

"What do you want, to expel my son?" my
mother asked in a low voice.

The man shook his head, pursed his lips, and
said nothing. Instead, he pulled out the fourth page
and placed it in front of my father and mother. My
mother seemed reluctant to pick up this paper again,
afraid that its shaking would betray her erratic
heartbeat. It was a photocopy of a newspaper—it
seemed to be about some high-ranking official
"visiting" the school, with a close-up of him and the
man in an intimate pose. He then spoke a string of
words I could not understand—my ears felt deaf,
yet I could hear the wind blowing through the grass
around me. My mother's expression shifted from
fear to confusion, to anger, to contempt, finally

blending all these emotions together; my father's face showed calmness before turning to fear like my mother's initial expression. The other "me's" eyes were blazing with glaring fury, just like the light radiating from the lotus pods' faces.

Anger is blinding, but no one notices its presence until it explodes. Every cell in my body urged the other "me" to react, but he did not. I thought, maybe I did not know what reaction would be appropriate either—perhaps no reaction was the best reaction. The man then pointed to the next page; this time, he did not casually tap on it but etched a deep underline under a sentence with his thumbnail:

"Spreading rumors can be punishable by death according to the law."

Before my parents could react, he pulled out two crumpled sheets of paper from his pocket. He slowly unfolded them, spreading one on each side in front of my parents. They were two certificates of psychiatric evaluation, and under the "Patient" field, my parents' names were boldly written.

The man smiled. Fire kindled in my father's eyes—it was a raging inferno; I saw anger refined into fuel and sarcasm turned into oxygen, and their meeting created a blaze capable of devouring everything. The man then carved another line under the words "death penalty" and knocked on these words several times with his knuckles. The bald man and the fat man grabbed my father's arms and forced him back onto the sofa as he tried to stand up. My mother also tried to say something but was restrained by the man in black and the flushed-faced man, just as the other two men held my father.

Sarcasm flashed in the man's eyes as well. He raised his right hand and issued orders to his subordinates. The bald man, the flushed-faced man, and the woman then went to different rooms while he moved to one side, firmly controlling the other "me." They rummaged recklessly through the bedroom, kitchen, bathroom, and balcony, not knowing what they were searching for. Everything in the house that looked like a box was opened, and every drawer was looted.

The chisel was indifferent to this scene. It focused intently on carving words on the wall, wiping them away, and carving new ones repeatedly. I saw it erase the "4" it had just written and meticulously engraved a "3," carefully smoothing every detail. It gently scooped up the fallen plaster dust from the floor, fixing the parts of the carving it found unsatisfactory.

"The next number is '2,' right?" I asked it, but it did not answer. So I asked again:

"What will happen when you write '0'?"

It continued its work, not looking back as it answered me:

"Wait. When the end of time comes, perhaps I

will enter your body, or perhaps I will leave for good."

No one in the room paid any attention to the chisel's flamboyant actions.

The fat man came out of my parents' bedroom at that moment, looking pleased as he glanced at the man. His hands stayed in his pockets, lovingly fiddling with the items inside. I could not see what those items were through his clothes, but I was sure they were heavy. The thin pockets trembled under the teasing of his fingers, as if they might break at any moment under the weight of the things trapped inside. The woman brought a chair from the study, carefully stood on it, and found a small box on top of the bookshelf. She opened it, and her eyes were filled with affection. Then she pulled out a black plastic bag that had been compressed to the extreme, shook it open in the air, and placed the small box inside. After tidying up the bag, she continued to pull a cylindrical roll from the bookcase, clamping it under her arm and quickly exiting the room.

The flushed-faced man stared blankly at the mess all over the floor. After a while, he lifted the empty drawer and smashed it hard on the ground. He leaned against the wall, his eyes full of disappointment, as if he had found nothing. The other "me" heard the noise, broke free from the man's grasp, and rushed into the room, too shocked to speak. The expression of surprise on his face lasted only a second before turning into rage. Tears welled up in his eyes, falling onto his feet.

The flushed-faced man approached the other "me," but not to speak with him; rather, he seemed intent on passing by him to leave the room. At that moment, I caught a whiff of an unusual smell—I could not describe it, but it felt like a mixture of many substances—alcohol, sweat, tears, adrenaline; these odors filled my nostrils, making my head throb painfully.

"That's called courage, and also recklessness," said the chisel. I saw that its work seemed to be nearing completion. This time, it quickly and carelessly carved the number "1"—it did not take the time to refine each detail of the digit but merely drew a vertical line. I realized that time seemed to be fast approaching its end.

After the chisel finished its work, it looked at me and then pointed with its tip to the other "me" and the flushed-faced man in the room. Everything happened so quickly—the other "me" suddenly grabbed the flushed-faced man, wrestling with him. I had never realized that the other "me" possessed such strength, like a charging rhinoceros, a runaway truck, or a bullet shot out of a gun. The struggle between the flushed-faced man and the other "me" felt like an earthquake, shaking the entire room to its core. The flushed-faced man tore through the window glass as if it were a sheet of paper, and at that moment, the other "me" fell silent. He stepped out of the broken shards of glass, moving like a falling leaf, stumbling as he walked down the air-formed steps, one step at a time, until he reached the ground.

I muttered to myself, "She will come soon, will not she?"

"Not yet. Remember, wait," the chisel responded. It had already drawn the "0," and the dust that had accumulated in the corner was scraped away and thrown out the window, following the other "me" to the ground. I thought, perhaps this is the end of time. But no one stopped moving; time seemed to be flowing faster and faster. The man and his subordinates appeared in the hallway, except for the woman, who got into the black van they had arrived in. She lowered her head, holding the black plastic bag in her hands, opening it eagerly, like a bride on her wedding day taking a brand-new diamond ring from her jewelry box.

The moment the woman closed the box, blue and white flowers bloomed all over the black car, and the wedding march began to play. A crowd gathered to watch. At that moment, the stream rushed toward me; it carried my small boat and stopped in front of me. Almost involuntarily, I got into the boat, and the stream continued to stretch forward. As I moved along with the current, I occasionally looked back, only to see the house carrying my father and mother growing farther and farther away.

III

I waved goodbye to the house. Sitting at the bow, I suddenly thought and asked it:

"If separation is destined, then why do we meet at all?"

Without hesitation, it replied, "Meeting and separation happen simultaneously."

For a moment, I lay on the slowly drifting boat and saw that the lotus pods just turned white, once again emitting yellow light from their holes. They summoned the chisel and brought along several eyeballs and a few masks that swayed before me. The stream could not speak but only made a dripping sound. I turned toward the sound and saw that the water was sometimes calm and sometimes rippled violently. These water waves were unlike anything I had ever seen—they were no longer colorless, transparent liquid but rather colorful, rigid solids. They moved along irregular paths, sometimes coming close to me, sometimes drifting away. But their absurd performance did not stir any emotions within me. Seeing that I ignored them, they left. Then a piece of music rang in my ears, and a voice told me:

"You are tired. Sleep now. Music may no longer be able to save you."

The music was most likely flowing from my girlfriend's fingertips, but the voice was not hers.

Suddenly, everything before my eyes went pitch black; I could not see a thing. I thought, "Might as well sleep, since I do not know what else I can do."

I was not sure if I fell asleep—perhaps I did, as I completely lost track of time; perhaps not, because I could still hear faint sounds, but the boundless darkness left me unable to determine whether my eyes were open or closed. When I awoke from my sleep—or perhaps when I was saved by someone from the darkness—I felt a warm sensation in my palm, as if it was this warmth that brought light back to me. Everything around me slowly brightened, allowing me to use my eyes again.

The warmth came from a freshly baked bun in my hand. My nose was busy trying to discern each ingredient in the bun, while my eyes scanned my surroundings in shock. I saw the bustling entrance of a school, the smoky snack stalls, the crowded shops, rows of streetlights, and a bus pulling into the station in a hurry. The stream and the little boat that had led me wandering all over were gone, and the ground beneath me was a vast expanse of hard concrete. I slowly placed the bun in front of my chest, and my girlfriend's face appeared before me. Her smiling eyes stared straight at me, but my mind was elsewhere, searching everywhere for the other "me."

"How is it? Does it taste good?" she asked.

I was startled. I thought she was speaking to

the other "me." But she took a step forward and gently touched my arm with the back of her hand. Only then did I realize she was talking to me. Nervously, I took a big bite of the bun, then handed it to her. I asked her to try it too, buying myself some time to continue looking for the other "me." The old lady who made the bun must not have spread the seasoning evenly; I took a big bite of rich sweet bean paste. My girlfriend tore off a piece and chewed slowly, muttering to herself that she was so hungry.

As she spoke, she glanced around, then hooked her arm through mine. Her wrist seemed electrified, and at the moment we touched, I was jolted awake by the current. The realness of her touch made me believe that the other "me" no longer existed—that I was both myself and the other "me." Relieved, I slowed my pace and walked with her. I tried to stretch out the time—this scene was too beautiful, and I feared it would vanish like a fleeting glimpse, never to come again in this lifetime.

"I remember your home is not in this direction," I suddenly recalled, noticing that she was walking further away from her house.

"It's Friday today; I'll walk you home," she said with a smile.

I nodded silently, but a smile crept uncontrollably to my lips. She kept her arm linked with mine and gripped it more tightly. I teased her, asking if she was afraid I'd run away. Tears welled up in her eyes, but she smiled and said yes. I told her I would not run, that I'd just keep walking with her, always walking together. I remembered that she once called me a rational person—indeed, how could I have thought of a word like "forever"? It's too absolute, and now it seemed all I could do was hold her hand and keep walking forward.

Every time we encountered a stranger on the street, I felt an impulse—I wanted to stop every stranger and tell them that the girl beside me was my lover. I loved her and wished to love her forever. But then I had an urge to mock myself for being childish—the word "lover" is a captive term; without the consent of others, it has no place in this world. No one believes in eternal love; they will only take my words as childish nonsense. So I compromised and told her, "I am willing to love you until death." She answered, "So am I."

The school gate grew farther away, and the bun in my hand became smaller. She said she felt a bit tired, so I led her to a bench at a nearby bus stop to sit down and casually tossed the plastic bag that had wrapped the bun into the trash can. The bag fell straight to the bottom of the bin, and I suddenly felt a sense of unreality. I rubbed my eyes and sat beside her again. She scooted closer to me until our thighs touched. Our school uniforms rubbed against each other, making a sharp, scratchy noise. She complained that the uniforms were of such poor quality—they had already torn in several places after only two years of wear. I said, "Anyway, we will not wear them after graduation; they are not even fit to be rags."

She agreed and added that it was not surprising the uniforms were bad, given that even the school's buildings were barely holding up. I wanted to continue with this topic, but she quickly covered my mouth with her hand, signaling me to stop talking. Her gesture brought the smell of the bun still lingering on her hand to my nose; the scent seemed to suppress my urge to continue the conversation, so I wisely dropped the topic.

Soon, she regained some of her strength and got up to continue walking, while I felt no fatigue at all. I remembered that when the bun had still been whole, the setting sun in the distance had cast a glow over her face, making her look more radiant than usual; now, only the pale moonlight filled the world, mingled with pink light[3] escaping from the rooms by the roadside, shining on the scantily clad women on the streets. Night had fallen, but she showed no intention of turning back home. I asked what her plans were; she thought for a moment and replied resolutely:

"I want to marry you."

I had meant to ask what her plans were for tonight. I was about to laugh at her misunderstanding, but I was stunned, feeling helpless and sorrowful all at once. I stopped the laughter that was about to escape and pointed to the women on the roadside. I told her, somewhat somberly, that these women had to come out and attract customers because they lacked sufficient allure, so they had to take the initiative, whereas love was different: it drew everyone in, so spoken love always seemed abrupt. As for a deeper reason, in my view, it was nothing more than different expectations. Men's expectations of prostitutes were for a brief, minute-long so-called "love," while what people truly hoped for was eternal love, but clearly, the possibility of failure was also great. It is precisely because it is so hard to attain that everyone desires it so much.

"You are always so pessimistic," she said.

I had no idea where this thought came from, and it startled me—I feared that either one of us might lose our expectations for love and marriage in the future, but I was also glad that it hadn't happened yet. I pondered for a moment and argued that pessimism is a reflection of optimism, and optimism is a reflection of pessimism. Pessimism arises from hope for the future, leading us to predict the bad things that might happen. In this way, people try to find ways to avoid future risks so they can have a beautiful future—it's a form of self-protection. Optimism, on the other hand, comes from a pessimistic view of the past, imagining a brighter future so that the past's suffering does not seep into one's soul—this too is a form of self-protection.

She shook her head with a smile, admitting she did not understand. I laughed too, put my arm around her waist, and we continued walking. This conversation seemed to last for a long time—I watched the moon rise and set, then allowed the sun's fresh rays to stick to my back. We passed by my house, and I invited her in. She was shy and hesitant, so I took her hand and confidently opened the door.

Both my father and mother were home, and the table was already full of dishes. The heavy iron door and tightly closed windows trapped the aroma of the food in the small house. My mother was in the kitchen, finishing the final touches. When she saw I was home, she hurried out, wiping her wet hands on her apron. My father, who had been practicing calligraphy in the study, put down his brush and invited my girlfriend and me to the table. My girlfriend's expression shifted from nervousness to apprehension, and she stood rigidly in place until I led her to a chair and asked her to sit down.

She looked at the delicious dishes in front of her but did not dare to pick up her chopsticks. My mother, in her hospitality, introduced each dish she had just prepared, and with each introduction, she put a piece on my girlfriend's plate. Only then did my girlfriend pick up her chopsticks, nodding repeatedly to express her gratitude. I could tell she loved my mother's cooking. My father, who knew nothing about cooking, seemed to want to make an effort too, seeing my mother's enthusiasm. So he turned to the kitchen, fetched a case of beer, and opened a bottle for my girlfriend and me. This time, she did not refuse. The bubbles from the beer exploded in her throat, making her unable to speak. After half a bottle, her face turned red—a natural blush more beautiful than any carefully applied makeup.

In truth, I felt more nervous than she did—this was my home, but I could not relax. I hadn't seen such a warm scene the last time I was here. So, I put down my chopsticks and walked to the window, noticing the intact glass. Then I went to the liquor cabinet and found my father's unopened bottles, climbed up to the bookshelf, and saw that the small box and the scroll were lying there quietly. My father's paperweight rested on the left side of his freshly copied phrase, "Life and death are both great matters," with the inkstone sitting proudly on the right side of the rice paper. Everything was so peaceful. I thought, perhaps everything I saw before was just a dream, or maybe this is a dream—or maybe it's all been a dream from the start.

My girlfriend and I left the house, both of us

belching from being so full. I told my parents we were going for a walk, and they happily bid us goodbye. My mother got up again, put her apron back on, and began tidying the dishes and placing them in the sink. My father returned to his study to continue his calligraphy. I thought, that's good, we should enjoy this beautiful leisure time. We did not take the same route back but continued moving forward, as if our subconscious had told us that going forward would make time pass more slowly.

However, I did not expect that moving forward would bring us to my girlfriend's building—I had assumed she would have to retrace her steps to get home. She seemed surprised too and took the opportunity to invite me to her place. Seeing my hesitation, she mimicked me from earlier, firmly grasping my hand and pulling me into the dark stairwell. I followed her steps up the stairs, and she fumbled in her pocket for her keys, unlocking the door in the darkness. When she turned on all the lights, I realized how unfamiliar everything was— this was the woman I loved deeply, yet I had never been to her private space. I proudly imagined that my presence would warm her cold bed, clean the unused plastic chairs, and open the rusty iron door in her heart.

She said she wanted to play a piece for me. I sat on the edge of her bed, watching her delicate hands slowly lift the piano lid. I tried to make time pass more slowly, fervently praying that the fleeting moments would allow me to remember every detail of what was happening. She seemed to sense my prayer and played a gentle piano melody. I vaguely felt that I had heard this piece before, and not just once. Music is like that—even the same piece, played by the same person, can evoke completely different feelings—it can be colored by the emotions of the moment, by unintentional mistakes, or even by the unrelated weather and environment, transforming it into something unrecognizable.

When the piece ended, she turned to me and asked, "Do you remember what you looked like the first time you heard me play the piano?"

I could not answer that question. She began to help me recall: the first time she played this song, it was merely to show off her skills, and I casually said it sounded good; the second time, I listened carefully and nodded, praising her technique; but this time, I was overwhelmed with emotion, my eyes brimming with tears. She asked me what I heard this time. I thought about it, tried to remember every note she played, and answered, "I heard flocks of sheep on a vast grassland, knights attending an investiture ceremony, thick ink flowing from a pen, gold and silver jewels covering the ground, and lovers accidentally meeting on a wooden spiral staircase." Clearly, my interpretation was far removed from the composer's original intent.

She responded with a smile—not one of mockery but of agreement. She got up, put on her ill-fitting school uniform again, took my hand, and pulled me up from the sofa. She said it was still early, and we should go for another walk. I was about to protest, but she opened the curtains, showing me the sun high in the sky. She used all her strength to push open the glass window and invited me to step out. I do not like the feeling of falling, so I asked her why we could not leave through the door. She said:

"Sometimes, we do not have the right to dislike the path we must take."

We did not fall straight down; instead, we descended step by step in a spinning motion onto the concrete road, yet the weightlessness of free fall was undeniably real. I dusted off myself and her, then asked where she wanted to go. She smiled without speaking, simply pulling me forward, as if something wonderful awaited us ahead. We passed by all the familiar sights, following a path so well-known it seemed etched in our bones, until we reached a brick wall.

She leaned against the wall, twisted open a bottle of drink, and handed it to me. This truly was a good spot. On both sides of the brick wall stood two symmetrical trees, their lush branches and leaves shielding us from the blazing sun. The scene

was so familiar, it felt almost foreign—I
remembered we had once received mosquito kisses
under their canopy, but today was the first time I
noticed that the roots of the two trees were quietly
creeping toward each other, slowly embracing. I
cheered for them—for finally meeting each other.
Their shoulders sheltered each other's toes from the
scorching sun and heavy rain, even as their trunks
were sinking into the dark and unknown soil.

My girlfriend looked up, admiring the smile on
the trees' brows. Seeing her, the trees shyly and
hurriedly stopped their laughter and fell silent. She
commented on their inability to meet freely and
praised their courage to defy fate. She held my
hand, showing off beneath the trees. My heart began
to beat irregularly again—it told me that everyone
around us was watching. I caught a glimpse of their
gazes and felt a bit nervous, but my girlfriend
looked at the two trees and said that many people
had once mocked their efforts, but they still
managed to come together. We can admire the trees,
so why cannot we accept the gazes of others?
People's eyes might hold ridicule, surprise, envy, or
praise, but what difference does it make to us?
Others might use us as a topic for idle gossip, but
that's all it would ever be.

Her words comforted me. I realized that we
were like the two trees she had mentioned. I held
her hand tightly, as if by doing so, I could absorb

her thoughts into my soul. She pulled me out from the shade of the trees, continuing toward the direction of the school. She pointed to a dense crowd dressed in blue and white ahead, then began to run with me, just as she had run from her house to mine before.

The wind filled the sleeves of her school uniform and made her slender arms invisible to outsiders. Her backpack bounced up and down in sync with my heartbeat. When we reached the crowd, she slowed down and guided me into it. The wind slipped out from her sleeves, and her backpack and my heart gradually calmed. She held my hand, gently parting the crowd. I kept hearing people calling my name, but when I looked around, I could not see any eyes directly meeting mine or any mouths that were open. I did not know how long we walked; the crowd seemed endless. Among the people we brushed past, some were familiar, some we had met once, and others we could not name. In the distance, it seemed like someone was shouting my girlfriend's name. I urged her to find out who it was, but she remained unconcerned, continuing straight ahead and saying:

"Loneliness is the true essence of life."

The sun seemed to have been lingering overhead for a long time. Only when we had pushed through the crowd, leaving everyone behind, did the sun begin to move slightly. At this moment, what lay before us was no longer the steel and concrete of the city but an endless green meadow. I opened my nostrils, letting the grass-scented wind drift into my mind. We no longer ran but walked slowly along the stream that bordered the grassland. The stream sometimes flowed gently and sometimes surged, with water droplets brushing against the rocks on the shore, creating a music-like sound.

In the vast expanse of grass, there was a solitary tree. It stood tall, its lush branches greeting the sun. My girlfriend and I walked hand in hand across the grass to rest beneath its canopy. The tree emitted a faint fragrance that smelled like intoxicating wine, delicate white orchids, fresh blood, pure steel, and burnt-out tobacco. We sat on the protruding roots, letting her head slowly rest on my shoulder and then move to my lap. The warm sun lulled her, and her eyelids gradually closed over her eyes. Before long, the tree playfully let a few rays of sunlight through, gently waking her.

She rubbed her eyes and, teasing the tree, asked why it stood here so alone, why it had no companions by its side. The tree did not answer but pointed its branches toward a distant flock of cattle and sheep. I saw them grazing leisurely, and a shepherd dog stared intently at the flock. I waved and greeted the dog, which looked in my direction and gently wagged its tail. Ants on the ground busily moved around me, marching in a line toward their home. I gently patted my girlfriend's head resting on my lap, my fingers brushing over the skin of her arm and stomach, as if soothing a baby to sleep. I did not know how long this scene lasted— maybe it had been a long time, but to me, it felt like a moment; maybe it was just a moment, but I was so immersed in this sweet moment that I forgot the passage of time. Yet, I still hoped I could hold her in my arms forever, letting her lean on me, her smile and spirit warming my life.

But alas, the moments that we cherish the most are the ones most easily carried away by the wind— it seemed as if we had just escaped from the crowd in blue and white to reach this meadow, but the crowd appeared again in the distance. They emerged from a small temple on the hillside, splitting into two groups: one dressed in neat black clothes, the other in strange white garments, both advancing rapidly toward us. I listened closely to the sounds of the approaching crowd, while she clung tightly to my hand and, before the crowd arrived, told me:

"I love you, until death."

"But staying alive is better, my dear," I replied.

She seemed to realize something. She looked at the solitary tree beside her, then into my eyes, and said:

"Perhaps we are destined to part. Perhaps it is now."

I felt as if I had known she would say this, and my heart did not stir. I stretched lazily, gazing down at her rosy, fair face, then looked at the crowd approaching from afar and mustered the courage to ask her:

"If separation is destined, then why did we meet?"

She hugged me and answered softly but firmly:

"If separation is destined, then meeting is also destined."

I closed my eyes in contentment—I think we had both found the answer we were looking for.

The Ivory Pendant in the Painting

I

If I spent the night in a hotel, I never drew the curtains. After turning off the lights, I liked to lie on the bed and look at the sky outside—sometimes, the night was dotted with stars, mingling with the scattered neon lights of the city; other times, it was raining or storming, and at those times, the sky actually felt brighter to me, as if the stars and the sea had reversed roles. What an interesting sight.

In those moments, I was usually completely naked. My skin pressed against the fresh, unfamiliar sheets and mattress, and my thoughts wandered and scattered along the fibers of the bedding. Occasionally, I felt the urge to reach for the cigarette on the nightstand, but I never lit it. I was afraid the sparks from the cigarette would sever the thread of my thoughts. Often, I turned my head to the side and looked at the woman beside me. Each time I did, it felt like a gamble—she might be facing me, lying on her side, fast asleep; she might have her eyes open, smiling at me, her cleavage subtly visible; or she might be turned away, the moonlight shining on her back, giving her skin a soft glow.

She was forty years old that year, our school's art teacher. She was not my wife, and I was not her husband, but I might have known her better than her husband did. She liked to stand naked in front of a full-length mirror after taking a shower and then put on her sheer lingerie—so sheer that her nipples were clearly visible. It seemed she enjoyed the feeling of being watched by the mirror; for this reason, she had even shaved off her pubic hair, leaving herself completely exposed in the mirror.

She said, "I put on this lingerie for you. Do you like it?"

I certainly believed her, but I usually removed these barely-there coverings a few minutes later. Once, after making love, I said to her, "Have you seen Sanyu's paintings[4]? Only nudes are worth looking at." She laughed heartily, as if mocking my taste in art. Whenever she laughed like that, I forgot that my thoughts had ever been tangled up in her, like water in a small river finally finding its way to the sea. In those moments, I believed she loved not just the physical contact and friction between our bodies but also the deeper connection of our souls.

The pleasure of sex was extended by our post-coital conversations, and it was always like this. These conversations took place in various settings: sometimes we lay on the bed, I held her, her head resting on my shoulder, her smooth breasts pressed against my chest; sometimes I sat on the hotel room's sofa or lounge chair, and she sat on my lap, and I felt the warmth of her body with my not-so-sensitive thighs. Often, as I listened to her speak playfully and provocatively, my thoughts wandered away, irresistibly.

"Did she ever imagine what it was like when I made love to my wife?"

This was the question I often asked myself in those moments. Since it was a question to myself, I sometimes gave contradictory answers:

"Of course she did. Who does not have an imagination?"

"No, she would not. She enjoyed our lovemaking, so why would she think about that?"

And then, this counter-question created new questions. I also wondered whether I should tell her that my original wife and I had long stopped having sex, but I always dissuaded myself. I kept telling myself not to overthink, much less to speak out; I was much older than she was, and since we weren't born at the right time, we should just enjoy the present. However, this self-admonishment always happened after the question had already formed in my mind. But we both had families; we were both trapped in the same cage. This cage might have been as luxurious as the Louvre, but it was still a prison; if we did not feel the helplessness of imprisonment for the moment, then there must have been a set of shackles and handcuffs quietly crawling up our limbs. She seemed luckier than me—her heart had long expelled her husband, leaving only room for me, so she was free of distractions; whereas I was a man, needing to provide for my wife, face a rebellious son, and, as the principal, deal with the school's complicated affairs.

She might also be part of those affairs. I never pursued her like a schoolboy—no fancy cars or mansions, not even candlelit dinners and flowers— our relationship was like two teenagers secretly dating, so pure that it could not be measured by the money that adults are familiar with. When I was with her, sometimes I suddenly trembled like a startled wild horse—at that moment, I realize that, just for a brief instant, I had forgotten my son, who was away at college but only plays video games, and my wife, who wears long-sleeved pajamas every night and turns her back to me in bed. After that moment, I would fall into deep self-doubt: What did I do wrong before? What am I doing now? What should I do in the future? I gave myself many answers, but none of them seemed correct.

I remember one night I spent with her: I held her and lost the battle against drowsiness, and then a series of strange dreams flooded my mind. In that dream, I stood on a beach, facing the sea, and an old wooden warship sailed toward me. When the old ship reached the shore, I saw my old friends disembark. They dragged me onto the ship, dusted me off, and made me stand tall. I stared blankly at everything; no one had taught me how to react. My friends clambered up the masts, hoisted the black sails, and respectfully called me "Commander." I stood on the deck alongside the large yellow dog I had raised as a child, watching it all unfold—I asked questions in bewilderment, while the dog wagged its tail at everyone.

When I woke up, the dream ceased to exist. I attributed its source to three things: I had recently watched a war movie, one of my close friends had recently died in a car accident, and I had never liked studying much as a child but always longed to become a soldier, especially a sailor. Unfortunately, my father insisted that I had to study and go to college; I could not end up in the military like my brother. He said, "The three brothers of the Zhuge family served Wei, Shu, and Wu; Lü Bu pledged allegiance to Ding Yuan, Dong Zhuo, and Wang Yun—our ancestors knew better than to tie themselves to one tree[5]."

But I still believed that sailing the seas would be the shining moment of my life—the sense of freedom, fulfillment, honor, and security was something the confines of my office can never provide. But she gave me that feeling; thus, I became even more obsessed with the time I spent with her. I once shared my dreams and feelings with her; she first told me that I was someone who valued loyalty and honor deep down and wanted to show my strength. Then she added that this emotion born out of thin air is what we call art, and the process of creating such emotions is creation—reality gives rise to emotions, emotions influence art, and art, in turn, nourishes reality.

I pondered her words, and she laughed again—she was laughing at my ability to understand. Sometimes, I want to laugh at myself: my background is in history, which emphasizes truth, while hers is in art, where truth is secondary. She said, "People only believe what they want to believe, and art is what people want to believe—it's like those famous paintings where the content is often imaginary, reflecting reality or using real objects to express unseen emotions. In any case, there are always some elements in a painting that are not real. And how do people measure the value of art? Simple, with money. The higher the 'artistic value,' the more expensive it is."

This gave me a new understanding of money. But I immediately asked her a question: "How much should a priceless treasure be worth? Who defines its price and value?" In my opinion, if a painting can be sold for a billion, it could just as well sell for ten billion; a painting that could be priced at ten billion being sold for only a billion would not seem unreasonable. She replied, "If something worth one dollar is priced at ten dollars, that's just greed on the merchant's part; if you can arbitrarily add or subtract zeros to the price of an artwork worth billions, that's power. Power is more attractive than money because power can always be exchanged for money, while money only has an eighty percent chance of buying power."

I said, "That's not quite right—power can be traded for money and beauty, money can buy power and beauty, and beauty can exchange for money and power. It's a triangle." She smiled and surprisingly praised my statement, while I fell into contemplation and could not help asking her if what she liked was my power, my money, or my looks. She transitioned her expression into a hearty laugh and replied:

"Your looks do not count, your power is not great, and money—you haven't given me any."

I did not know if our relationship was like a game. Some people think a game is just a game; people play it for fun. But others get so immersed that they blur the lines between reality and virtuality. For me, sometimes, it did feel like a game, because I ultimately had to return to my family and life. At the same time, it did not feel like a game because the physical and psychological pleasures were so real and linger for a long time. Her post-coital conversations often added to her charm in my mind, a charm I had never found in other women—sometimes, her thoughts, casually revealed in her words, prompted me to reflect on myself and conducted a meticulous self-examination: Do I love my wife? When did my son start being rebellious, and what triggered it? What traits of hers match mine, and which ones clash? I had never given myself a definite answer and instead found myself trapped in a whirlpool where memories and introspection alternated. I had a childhood sweetheart as a young man; she came from a good family, but we lost touch after parting ways until I heard she had married someone else. My wife was a hometown acquaintance; we met by chance, married by chance, and had a child by chance. At that time, I subconsciously believed life should be like this—if fate had decreed I spend my days with a stranger until death, so be it. Then, I met her. By the time I first met her, I was already an old teacher, and she was a fresh university graduate. When I met this polite young woman, I could not help but feel a liking for her, but unlike our current relationship, I only felt an inexplicable attraction.

Even now, I am still a fatalist. In my heart, everything I have experienced is due to fate—the moment I met her and every night we spent together were gifts from fate; my friends were fate's support, and my marriage and son were fate's momentary lapse, while my son's rebellion was a joke played by fate.

But this joke seemed a bit over the top. I often find myself in a daze, realizing that the same scene keeps playing out: my wife and I lie in bed; she turns her back to me, seemingly asleep, while a vast distance separates us. At this point, scenes from my son's growth repeatedly replay in my mind—it seemed as if this bed was not a place for sleep. In my memory, my son, when born, was like a precious gift bestowed by the god. At that time, the whole family had no doubt that he was the family's hope, destined to become exceptional. My wife and I took care of him with the utmost attention, and his intelligent eyes were a light in my life. The next scene jumped straight to when he had just started elementary school. He was very naughty then; my father, his grandfather, did not see anything wrong with it. He would buy snacks and toys for his grandson and take him on outings. Admittedly, I was busy with work then and could not give him the attention he needed, and by the time I realized it, my young son had already become a child who did not want to do his homework.

Then, it seems my memory has a gap—I've already forgotten how my son spent the three years from ages three to six. I think, "It is just kindergarten; nothing important. It's in elementary school that he should start studying seriously." Until one day, when relatives came to visit and said to my son, who was in his final year of kindergarten:

"In September[6], you'll have to start doing your homework properly."

My son burst into tears. His cry was like a heavy hammer striking my head and heart. Though it did not shatter me completely, it filled me with a sense of suffocation and pain. His reaction was not exaggerated, nor was it a baseless cry; he was just a child who could not suppress his emotions subtly, who could only let his raw fear for the next stage of life spill out. The relatives' faces showed a mix of bewilderment, disdain, and indifference—some continued drinking and chatting, not caring about a child's reaction at all. I had never imagined such a thing could happen to me; I always prided myself on being a teacher at a prestigious high school, a title that was quite impressive and respected at the time. Many called me a "famous teacher," and I gradually got used to this piercing title. To me, it was like a dazzling yet heavy crown, revered by everyone but hiding the flesh and blood beneath. Underneath the crown, it felt like a blade had pierced my brain; if it were pulled out, I would immediately lose my memory or even die—I had to wear this crown, for it was my dignity, even my life.

From that moment on, time seemed to come at me even more fiercely. I tried to stop it, to conquer it, to make it slow down, but it never did. Instead, it turned from a straight line into a circle—every day with my son felt like a repetition; I urged him to study, and he stubbornly refused. Then I forced him, and he resisted. Occasionally, I would have a thought: If I had really joined the navy back then, would I have found some excuse for myself? For instance, my son has the same stubbornness as I do, like a soldier who follows orders resolutely, with only two possible outcomes: death or victory.

Whenever I think of this in the dead of night, I turn to look at my wife's sleeping back; this glance carries my thoughts further—either moving forward, imagining the road ahead and getting lost in confusion, or moving backward, replaying the path we've traveled over the years, only to find myself mired in the same confusion. And when I feel lost, I suddenly understand my son's bewilderment—a child cannot be smooth and subtle in this world, cannot gracefully stop sighing, cannot remain calm in front of ruthless test papers, and cannot smile brightly amid a crowd that mocks him. No one, including me, can tolerate a defense for poor grades on a test, because at that moment, whether it's a reasoned, impassioned argument, an effort to flatter those judging him, or an outburst of emotion, all these behaviors are simply categorized as the unreasonable excuses of a societal misfit.

When I was a child, my family kept several big yellow dogs. In winter nights, I would slowly tuck my freezing feet under their bellies, and they would gladly offer me a little warmth. They would bark loudly to drive away strangers, guarding the small, poor village that was my home. But suddenly, at some point, I seemed to have become someone afraid of a dog's bark; or rather, it was not just fear, but a mix of fear and disgust. Once, I heard a neighbor's dog barking frantically in the middle of the night, and I impatiently opened my eyes, praying for it to stop—but it did not. So, I got up from the bed, went to the living room, and was shocked to find the front door ajar. Nervously, I pushed open my son's bedroom door, reached out to pull back his blanket, only to touch a cold pillow. The pillow's fibers carried static, piercing through the air and my nerves.

Finally, my wife and I found him in a bar, amidst the red and green lights. The distant dawn appeared on schedule, heralding the start of a new day; right in front of me, my son, surrounded by young, sexy girls, was telling me that what I thought was a future concern had already arrived. We brought him home, walking under the chaotic neon lights. On the way, I could not help but feel hatred toward everything—I hated that the bronze artifacts of Sanxingdui could not take me back in time, that Su Dongpo's poetry hadn't created a perfect world, and that the complicated physics formulas had never cared about my feelings.

We returned home with mixed emotions. My wife blamed my father for spoiling our son, blamed my absence, blamed my brother, who, after becoming a battalion commander, indulged in vices and corrupted our son. When bricks of hail fall from the sky, no one can help but protect their head or seek shelter—my wife's accusations were like hail, and my instinct for self-protection was instantly triggered. I leafed through my foggy memory from that time and could only recall my incoherent rebuttals. My rebuttals were weak; I tried to sustain my thin sense of confidence with shouts and yells.

Every time I recall this, I find it unbearable to continue, or rather, there is no point in continuing, because the days that followed were filled with endless arguments, as if nothing had ever changed. Not only did the arguments remain the same, but everything around me remained unchanged: my father still insisted that the child was young and continued to spoil him; my brother still held onto his lifestyle habits, but his steady rise through the ranks of the military silently influenced my son; my wife continued to blame me, my father, and my brother.

Nothing changed—except for the increasingly harsh judgment I placed on myself within my heart. I told myself that after struggling, one should accept fate, that right and wrong should be left for the future to decide. I advised myself not to dwell on these predestined questions—but then I asked myself, what should I dwell on? I had no answer, but whenever I thought of this question, I always recalled the rare moments I spent with my wife and son, sitting on the grass in the park by the lake. We laid a tablecloth on the grass, placed some snacks on it, and talked all afternoon. The grass, soaked with moisture, defiantly poked through the fabric, pricking us. In the distance, a few turtles occasionally came ashore to rest in the lake, and white water birds perched around us, ready to steal a piece of cake whenever we weren't looking. My son saw the little fish on the water's surface, opening their mouths to breathe, and wanted to catch them. I hurriedly called him back, and he remained curious, wondering why the little fish wanted to talk to him. Those beautiful moments were toxic; every time I tasted those memories, I felt as if I'd lost my mind, as if I might instantly transform from a genteel teacher into a crazed gorilla, pounding my chest in fury at everything around me. But sadly, I must suppress such impulses and maintain the image of a normal person.

When I had nothing to do, I often gazed out from my office on the top floor toward the playground below. I could see the boys happily playing soccer, the girls chatting and laughing, and the students stopping teachers in the corridor to discuss questions. All these scenes reminded me of the night I found my son. I could not vent my emotions—not there, where I had no right to do so. So, whenever I saw or thought of such joyous scenes, I felt a force tearing me apart—I closed my eyes and saw myself split in two, one half innocent and pure, humming lively or gentle tunes; the other half ferocious, baring bloody fangs and claws. I envied the world below—the laughter of young students was like the siren's song, while I was like a sailor on a treasure-laden naval warship, desperately resisting the deadly temptation, afraid of being drawn into the whirlpool of beauty. Sometimes, I blamed myself, for whenever I had free time, my internal monologue and leaps of thought increased, always filling my mind. I attributed this to my immaturity. I could not define maturity, but in my heart, maturity meant ignoring meaningless noise, not striving to change fate with extremism, not casually expressing lofty ambitions, and not venting grievances to those who could not help; like an apple that, when mature, would quietly fall to the ground, and in the end, everything returned to nothingness.

I was ultimately not a mature person, at least not the kind of mature person I imagined. Perhaps I would never become that mature apple because I was still enjoying the wind, frost, rain, and dew, still eagerly seeking the answers to every question in my life. I feared that in the process of seeking answers, I might lose direction and myself, but I persisted in convincing myself that no matter how my actions and thoughts changed, I would always remain me.

II

I once tried to sum up and evaluate my own life, but I came up with three different viewpoints:

"I was pushed into the present by my family's past."

"The past has never passed, and the future has already arrived. The past, present, and future are inseparable."

"There is no such thing as past or future. Everything is the present, and it can only be the present."

These three conflicting views often presented themselves simultaneously before me. I asked her once, "What kind of person do you think I am? Am I living in the past, present, or future?" She answered firmly, "The past." As soon as she gave that answer, I knew it was the one I liked least because I was hoping for either of the other two. Yet my subconscious told me this was the correct answer. I was certain this was the moment when our minds were most lucid: we lay in bed as we always did, letting the moonlight into the room, talking about everything under the sun. I asked her why she thought I was living in the past and what made her see that.

"That girl," she said, pouting playfully.

I gave an awkward laugh. I had once shown her a photo of a student and told her that there was a girl in the new class who looked just like her—or at least how I imagined she looked in her youth. I had also shown her a photo of my first love, whose features indeed bore some resemblance to hers. I asked if she was referring to my first love or the girl from our school. She told me she was talking about the girl at our school. I laughed, unsure whether it was out of embarrassment or because I felt a sense of her childishness.

She asked, "You haven't slept with her, have you?"

I instinctively answered, "No," but was suddenly surprised. She was smoking, and the white smoke, illuminated by the moonlight, streamed simultaneously from her nose and mouth, curling at her lips before floating into the air. I lit a cigarette too, letting the dull pleasure continue to fill my body. She got up from the bed, casually pulled a bath towel from the hotel closet, spread it out on the sofa, and sat down naked, pouring half a glass of whiskey into two cups—the whiskey was just brought back from the United States by her husband. She handed me a glass, looking at me with an inscrutable smile, as if hoping I would continue to talk about what had happened between me and that girl.

I decided to take a moment, to sort out my emotions. So I sat naked across from her, picked up the glass, sniffed it, and let a small sip of the liquid flow into my mouth. The whiskey was not to my taste; it tasted like rotting wood coated in varnish, then cut into pieces, shredded, and soaked in alcohol. My expression must have conveyed my feelings; she laughed and said:

"Things you've never tried always seem so appealing, but sometimes they just do not suit you—unless you've grown used to them."

I knew what she meant. A hypothetical scenario was arousing genuine jealousy in her, while her reason struggled to suppress it; when reason and jealousy collide, a chemical reaction called suspicion occurs, simultaneously eroding passion and producing hatred. From her confident expression, I could tell she thought she understood men well—at least, she thought she understood me. I also believed I understood women; with a bit of cunning, I could perceive her faint thoughts. She looked at me with a sly expression, as if proclaiming her victory. I smiled, took another sip of the whiskey, and shook my head, denying the thoughts in her mind.

But she might have just been making a small joke. After that, she did not mention the girl again, but the image of the girl remained firmly imprinted in my mind. Occasionally, I could see this girl—the younger version of her—from my office window. Sometimes, she would struggle to twist off the cap of a bottle in front of the school's snack shop;

sometimes, she would wear a short-sleeved shirt while playing badminton; other times, she would rush into the classroom when the bell rang. She always seemed to be alone, but she would walk with a boy after school. I could not remember what the boy looked like, nor did I know his name, but I could tell they seemed to like each other.

I was a bit envious of that boy. I often asked myself, if she and I were twenty years younger, would we be together? My answer to myself was clear: I would fall in love with her, but she was still young and probably would not marry me. I thought that twenty years ago, she must have lived a life similar to that of this girl. Being born at the wrong time is the seed of pain; its emergence has nothing to do with wealth, status, or identity. Once this seed is planted, it grows into a towering tree, and any joy is overshadowed by its shade of suffering. Thus, my envy and pain merged—I had to admit, I felt a tinge of jealousy toward that boy. I guess my jealousy might be similar to hers toward that girl.

But after all, I was the principal, and all I could do was gaze from my office window, silently imagining a beauty that never happened. I once asked my brother—who happened to be the homeroom teacher of that girl—if he allowed young love[7] among his students. Without a hint of hesitation, he firmly said, "No." That answer was not surprising, but I regretted asking the question as soon as it left my mouth, fearing he might connect it back to me. However, after he gave his answer, I could tell from his eyes that he hadn't thought much of it.

This conversation took place at a gathering of friends. She, my brother, a few of my friends whom I called brothers, and I were all there. These friends and I had been inseparable since university, and even when we started working, we taught at the same school. I was deeply grateful to them because their full support gave me the chance to become the principal—though my position was appointed by the higher-ups, their backing made it possible for me to fulfill the role. When I posed that question, I already knew that no matter his answer, I would support him because he was my brother.

He explained his reasoning, "When we were in high school, we were either studying or fooling around. The most rebellious thing we did was secretly smoke or drink. Back then, we never thought about falling in love, so dating is not necessary for today's students either. Furthermore, dating without the intention of marriage was a crime punishable by death in the past[8]; a crime remains a crime and does not become justifiable with time. The only difference today is that the government no longer drags young couples out to be shot—but that does not mean shooting them was wrong, nor does it mean early dating is right. It merely means the government and people are more tolerant now."

We seem to have equated young love with promiscuity. Another of my brothers also supported the stance against young love, though his reasoning was different. He waved his hand, asking everyone to quiet down, and so we all set aside our bowls, chopsticks, and glasses, listening attentively to what he had to say. He warned us solemnly that we represent the school, and banning young love is for our own good, not just for the students. If a girl gets pregnant, we, as teachers and the principal, will be held responsible—the parents may question why we did not notice the early signs of romance, why we did not stop it in time.

She added that if young love happens, the best outcome is that nothing happens; the second-best is a big incident, so big that we cannot handle it ourselves and the government or police must step in. The worst-case scenario is a minor incident, like a young couple being hit by a car or a girl getting pregnant.

"I believe if there were another 'Strike Hard' or 'Campaign against Spiritual Pollution,'[9] no one would oppose it," he continued. "Young love is, on the surface, an indulgence in hedonism, but at a deeper level, it is the result of being corrupted by capitalist ideology. This ideology cannot be left unchecked. To put it mildly, if these kids only focus on young love, they will not contribute to the country; to put it more seriously, unchecked, the result is a country that is no longer a country. To take it even further, China would become a colony of the Americans[10]. So this is not just about young love; this is national hatred and family enmity!" Everyone nodded, and it seemed our positions were strongly aligned. My brothers remarked that if we had joined the military back then instead of becoming teachers, we would surely have been loyal and fierce warriors of the Party, an indestructible force. After that, they temporarily set aside this serious topic and focused on praising me, saying I should have been their platoon leader instead of the principal. I was not unfamiliar or uncomfortable with such compliments; on the contrary, with my brothers, I was more willing to share my past dreams of being a soldier—whether strategizing and commanding thousands of troops or fighting alongside my brothers.

She, however, could not help but continue discussing the topic of students dating. The age difference between her and me seemed enough to create a generation gap, so in her words, there was never a mention of executing student couples—something I attributed to her not having formed a deep impression of that era. I never mentioned wanting to eliminate students in love either, but I clearly understood that this was because I did not want to put myself in the position of a death row inmate, nor did I believe that making love to her was a capital crime. However, our unspoken understanding provided me some comfort; at least I could be certain that our relationship would not make us think of death.

The end of a gathering is always filled with both a sense of melancholy and relief. I still remember that night; a gentle yet fierce rain poured down, its droplets either pounding heavily on the umbrellas or falling into uneven puddles. Her high heels tapped rhythmically on the pavement, the faint sounds of music echoed from a nearby dance hall, and people in the small eateries were burying their heads in plates of late-night snacks. She clung to my arm and sighed, saying how beautiful this scene was. I agreed, adding that it would be great to capture it in a painting. But then again, what difference would it make to paint this scene? It's just a fleeting illusion, with no way to prove it ever existed.

But she said she would paint it and give it to me once it was done.

I nodded. If there truly were such a painting, I would hope it depicted me, my wife, and our son, walking through the misty air from a barbecue stall, stepping over loose cobblestones; our son taller than both my wife and me, holding a giant umbrella big enough to shelter all three of us. That's why photography can never replace painting—there is so much that a camera cannot capture. I suppose there is no such giant umbrella in reality, but at this moment, it was just the two of us, and the umbrella we shared was just big enough to cover our shoulders as we walked toward the hotel.

She did not paint in the hotel room. As always, we were naked, only covered by the blanket. She lay sideways in my arms, talking about her longing for and understanding of art. She said that art is filled with nothingness, but the end of art is always reality; this has never changed. Even with completely incomprehensible abstract paintings, their foundation is reality, and their ultimate meaning is also reality. If there is no real meaning, the artwork will die, sinking forever in people's memories. If art is a table, then it is like a tablecloth spread over that table, but if the table itself is gone, then the tablecloth becomes useless.

"So, if I were to paint us tonight, I would not recreate tonight's scene like a camera would."

"How would you paint it, then?" I asked curiously.

She then began to describe the picture in her mind: On a vast ocean covered by dark clouds, I stand at the bow of a lonely warship, in front of a sea of soldiers with only my brothers wearing distinct uniforms. I raise my right hand, passionately delivering a pre-battle speech, telling everyone that we are fighting for honor. She stands beside me, dressed in a black trench coat and hat, her head bowed. In the distance, the sky is ablaze with fire, but on my ship, there is only the calm before the storm.

I asked her what this had to do with tonight's scene. She smiled silently at first, then, after lighting a cigarette, she told me that this scene contained my dreams, my dignity, my honor, my brothers, my love, and the reality of my life.

Her answer seemed to lift the cloth covering the table of art. I marveled at her understanding of me and even more at how she could use a single, still image to explain my current situation—with only brothers and a lover by my side, family life could hardly be considered satisfactory, much like a smoky, turbulent sea where crises seem distant yet ever-present. I did not dare continue asking her for more details about her envisioned painting, for fear she might stir up memories I would rather not recall.

"Your painting has a very Western style; my brother might have some opinions about that," I joked slightly.

She burst out laughing and told me, "A person, or even a society, holds different standards for different groups, just like nobody would expect you, as a principal, to be good at science and math. But our requirements for students are many: they have to study hard, follow the rules, respect teachers, avoid young love, and not eat snacks in class, and so on. Besides, your brother usually drives a German Audi, drinks French wine, and I saw him smoking Marlboro last time—you know that's a foreign brand, right?"

Her words relaxed me a little. So I returned to the previous topic and asked, "What kind of paintings do you like?"

"Expensive ones," she replied.

This was an answer I had never expected. I asked her why, and she answered that the value of a piece of art depends on two factors: one is time—a two-thousand-year-old artifact, regardless of its craftsmanship, even if it was just a chamber pot casually discarded back then, would still be valuable; the other is artistic achievement—its value lies in the universal recognition of its artistic depth, so even a layperson, unable to understand it, can perceive its worth through its price. Just like people, one's value comes from being recognized by others.

"Do you think I am recognized by others?"

"Some recognize you, some do not; some do not dare to openly refuse to recognize you, while others dare to."

Her answer sparked my curiosity. I had never been curious about how others praised me because I knew that praise was mostly insincere; no matter how flowery the words of praise, they meant nothing to me. So I asked her, who does not recognize me, and what do they disapprove of? As I asked this, I pondered various possibilities: was it my brothers disapproving of my relationship with her, were they jealous of my becoming the principal, had I been seen littering by a neighbor, had I criticized the clumsy hotel staff, or had I abandoned the dog my son had raised? I silently criticized myself for my reckless speculation, but my eyes instinctively turned to the window, hoping that the raindrops and lights outside would scatter my thoughts.

She calmly took a folded piece of paper from her handbag. I recognized the familiar scent of the paper—it was the mixture of the school's standard-issue printer paper and ink, with a hint of her perfume and body wash. Nervously, I took the paper from her hand—I did not know why I was so tense; I guessed it might have been because her envisioned painting had left a deep impression on me or perhaps even a psychological shadow. I had always believed that a man's life was about carefully balancing family and career, but now my wife and I were sharing a bed yet dreaming different dreams, and my son was estranged from me. I feared that when I opened this paper, my career would also be plunged into an abyss.

I do not remember how long it took to unfold that paper; it might have been a second, or it might have been ten minutes. This part of the memory seems deliberately erased by myself. But I remember how I persuaded myself to read the words on the paper—if I did not open it, I would remain stuck in confusion and fear, and others' disapproval of me would always exist; if I opened it, at least I could understand the situation, maybe even do something about it. Perhaps I still had a chance to reclaim the dignity I deserved.

As I read the content on the paper under the dim light of the hotel, my trembling hands became visibly shaky—the paper was a post, with some photos showing leaks in the columns and beams of the school's teaching building; beneath the photos was a sentence saying that the school would be ruined in my hands. For a moment, I was at a loss; perhaps anger filled my mind, or maybe I had never thought a student, younger than my son, would challenge my authority. I stared at the words on the paper for a long time, not knowing what to do.

The bedside lamp grew dimmer and dimmer. She said she had intended to tell me about this in the morning but feared I would not be in the mood to dine with my brothers and even more worried that I would not be in the right state for lovemaking tonight, so she chose this moment to bring it up. I thought this might be an excuse; had I not brought up the topic of "recognition," perhaps she would not have mentioned it. But now that I knew, her excuse no longer mattered, not to mention I could not be sure if she was telling the truth or making excuses.

People in love always end up begging or even pleading. Love itself is a form of begging—people beg for care and affection from each other, for beautiful memories, for financial favors, and for sexual satisfaction. And those in love cannot resist this begging; all reason and logic are destroyed in favor of fulfilling the plea. So, begging my lover for answers became my only option now—I silently begged her to comfort me at this moment, to calm me down. Perhaps she heard my inner call, or perhaps the time was right; she came over to sit beside me and gently said:

"Do not be angry."

These three words initially brought me comfort, but shortly after that brief relief, I started to mock my own fragility. That even such three words—words anyone could say—could comfort me, how long had it been since I last experienced this warmth? I tried to dig through my memories but could not recall the last time I felt this way. Maybe it was when my wife agreed to marry me, or perhaps when my son first called me "Dad"—but in any case, those moments felt so long ago that they seemed foreign to me. In retrospect, comforting actions always have some element of foolishness: I cannot really follow the advice to "not be angry," nor can I return to those beautiful moments in my memories, yet I was foolishly comforted.

After saying those three words, she paused for a long time, seemingly waiting for my reaction, but the frozen atmosphere made it impossible for me to focus on my next move. In a daze, I pulled the cushion on the sofa to my chest and hugged it tightly, hoping it would somehow suppress my chaotic thoughts. When I had calmed down a bit, I lit a cigarette and tried to ask her calmly:

"What do you think I should do?"

"Home visit."

I knew very well that as a principal, I should not ask such a question; instead, I should come up with a detailed plan and let my subordinates carry it out. When she gave her answer, I already had a top, middle, and bottom strategy in mind: the best strategy was to put pressure on the student's parents, make the student delete the post, and after some time, no one would remember this matter; the middle strategy was to talk directly to the student; the worst strategy was to let things take their course, taking one step at a time. Her answer coincided perfectly with my thoughts, except I hadn't yet decided exactly how and for what reasons to conduct the "home visit"—I was used to designing a comprehensive and detailed plan, like a movie director mapping out scenes or an excellent commander anticipating every move of the enemy. Meanwhile, she was like a strategist, laying out a grand plan for me, the commander, and helping me make a decision.

She outlined the necessity of this "home visit" that I had been anticipating. She said, "First of all, our school has been inspected by provincial leaders[11] and leaders from the Ministry of Education, and they have given our school high praise. Building a school is not just the school's responsibility; many departments at the city and provincial levels must participate. If we allow students to criticize the quality of the construction, it would embarrass the leaders, making us guilty of a political mistake, and in the end, everyone would use us as scapegoats. On the other hand, if we put pressure on the student and his parents, regardless of whether we succeed, it would be them committing the political crime, not us. Secondly, students are not professionals; they do not know how to assess building quality. If there is actually a problem with the building, you would be the one held primarily responsible; if the building is fine but just has some leaks, then we are allowing rumors to spread. So we must take control of this situation. Additionally, given the current climate of strict punishment for those who spread false information, it's okay for us to make a big deal out of a small matter, but we cannot afford to downplay a serious issue. Lastly, if we do not intervene, where will our authority be in the future? Neither students nor teachers will respect us anymore."

I laughed and remarked, "You've truly proven yourself from all those years of working for the Party and the Youth League[12]. You've hit the nail on the head."

She smiled too but then added seriously, "This is about your dignity and mine. Not only do we need to solve this issue, but we also need to make a big deal out of it. It does not matter if the matter escalates; the real risk is if it does not. Your brother told me, 'For people like this, we must treat them like the reactionary Nationalists, with bayonets drawn and ready to see blood.' There's some truth in what he says; after all, when something like this is elevated to a matter of national importance, it concerns the country's political security." From the look in her eyes, I could see her urgency. There was a hint of challenge in her urgency, as if to say, "We soldiers are ready to fight to the death; why is His Majesty thinking of surrendering first?" I flashed a naive smile and told her I would follow her lead and not let anyone down—there seemed to be a hint of gratitude in my promise to her; I was grateful for the expectations and trust she placed in me, grateful for my brothers' consideration, something I hadn't felt from my wife and son in a long time.

This was the most unusual work meeting I had ever conducted in my life: it was uniquely concise, without a prepared speech, without long-winded introductions, without distinctions between those on

stage and those in the audience, and even without
clothing—as if in our naked state, it was easier to
open our hearts and be honest with each other, and
easier for me to take a deeper look at myself. At that
moment, I was examining my own laziness: there
was a moment when I told myself, let it go, let this
matter pass; in a few years, I would retire anyway.
If this conversation were happening in a formal
setting, I would be more concerned about my attire,
or whether there were any typos in my speech, but I
would never put the content of the meeting first.

After that, I became keen on this concise style
of meeting—it captivated me. I walked into the
office in the morning light the next day and
gathered my subordinates to discuss our strategy.
My brother also took some time to come to my
office and join the discussion. Looking back now,
there was a certain chaotic beauty to that scene. Our
seating arrangement no longer had a hierarchy, and
what could be called a meeting had discarded the
so-called "traditional" processes and rules; around
us were desks and sofas, desks cluttered with dust-
covered lamps that hadn't been cleaned in ages,
along with books left casually open—these
elements, which would traditionally be seen as signs
of disorder, held a certain indescribable beauty in
my eyes.

This beauty, which I had never noticed before,
transformed into my motivation to act, validated the

legitimacy of my anger, solidified my wavering resolve, and celebrated my yet-undiscovered inner capabilities. Seeing the dust that had nowhere to hide under the lamp's light, I made up my mind.

III

The only thing that people can really boast of ignorance. Take me as an example—I imagine myself fighting alongside my brothers on a naval battleship, but I suppose real soldiers would have laughed at my ignorance. Or consider that boy—he knows nothing about what it takes to build a school, nor does he understand what honor and dignity mean to me. Yet he boasts about discovering a major hidden danger at the school, as if doing so would make him a hero saving countless people.

So, what was his motive for taking these photos? If he still had a chance to answer this question himself, I think he might say that everything he did was for everyone's safety and the justice in his heart. But I would not believe such an explanation. Perhaps he does have a bit of a sense of justice, but I am certain that justice is not the only reason—every person wants attention and support; that's the most direct reason. The most fundamental reason, however, is that when someone gains attention and support, they will receive tangible or intangible benefits. If it hadn't been for her reminder, or if I hadn't tried to examine myself and others more deeply, I would not have uncovered this reason. And after each self-examination, I feel I have gained a deeper self-awareness; I believe that a person with self-awareness often finds themselves to be a bundle of contradictions and conflicts. When I look back years later on the things I have done, I feel these contradictions within me becoming increasingly intense—I can meticulously prepare for an insignificant meeting yet neglect my son's childhood; I love my son yet am filled with hatred for his failings; I bravely punish students only because I fear the possible punishment from my superiors.

The painting she made for me was hung in my office. Just as she had envisioned, the painting depicts me, her, my brothers, the battleship, and the smoke-covered sea. I stare at this painting, as if returning to that rainy night. That day, after we ended our conversation, we each went home. My mind involuntarily began predicting every detail of what might happen next, every minute and second. I contemplated the potential variables: Would the student give in? Would the parents respond calmly, or would they react vehemently? How would my brothers treat the student and his parents?

As I walked down the street, I merged these variables into the imagined storyline. I pictured us arriving at the residential area on a sunny weekend, smiling and accepting the greetings of the students and parents, gently knocking on the student's door. The student's parents offered us tea and snacks, and I slowly explained the whole situation. In the end, we shook hands, the student deleted the post, the parents apologized, and we graciously forgave them. But I asked myself, would things really go so smoothly? So, I added these variables to the script I had just created. In this version, we walked into the residential area through misty air, insects in the grass seemed to leap in surprise. When we knocked on the door, the parents invited us in, but the student would have cursed us, and the parents would have been hostile to our arrival. Everything around us seemed filled with hostility, all working tirelessly to drive us away, as if even their sofas and coffee tables had sprouted legs and were brandishing gleaming knives at us. My brother, to protect us, fought with everything and everyone around.

"That thought is too extreme," I told myself, mocking my wild imagination. My imaginings were not over yet, but I had already reached my front door. It was late at night, and I carefully took out my key, trying not to make a sound. I slowly pushed the door open, but it still made a metallic scraping noise. When the noise stopped, everything returned to silence. The house was filled with a dead atmosphere—my wife was already lying on her side in bed, as always, with her back to the empty space left for me. The door to my son's room was open; he was not home, and I imagined him at a bar, holding a sixteen-year-old girl, drinking and having fun. But now, unlike before, I would not go out to search for him like an adult. Nothing seemed to have changed. I had tried to let go of my obsession with what the future held for my son, and it seemed I had indeed managed to let go for a short time. However, a person's life must have some focal points—family, friendship, love... I realized that when I could no longer focus on family, my attention to family was divided, sold off to friendship and love.

So, she, my brothers, and I set off. As I had expected, it was a sunny noon. Everyone's clothing and mental state were different, like the different stars and planets in a galaxy—some remained silent, quietly maintaining the stability of the entire system; others shone brightly, providing direction for the stars around them. When this thought crossed my mind, I felt like another Copernicus, perhaps even a greater figure than Copernicus—I realized I was the sun, and everyone revolved around me, while I provided them with the source of life. As the car door opened, the real sun appeared. I looked up at it—it was too bright to look at directly, so I squinted and quickly lowered my head. The students we encountered in the residential area acted no differently toward me than I did toward the real sun—some bowed their heads to greet me, trying to avoid eye contact, and even seemed unsure of how to move their lips, muttering "Hello, Principal" or "Hello, Teacher" from their throats. Some students pretended not to see us, even taking out their English books and nonchalantly memorizing vocabulary.

But none of that mattered. We lined up in a row and entered the narrow corridor, my brother at the front and I at the rear; according to him, the vanguard is made up of the most loyal warriors, while the backbone of the team stays in the rear. When we entered their door, the student's parents seemed to sense the unusual atmosphere—although they greeted us with smiles, they sat stiffly across from me with a coffee table between us, especially the father, who sat upright and silent. I leaned back on the sofa, my right hand resting diagonally on the armrest, scratching my earlobe, as if I were the one who should have been uneasy. The purpose of our encounter was ultimately for my benefit—I was the one making the demands, and whether they complied with my demands, I could not say for sure; I could not even determine whether they were fully under my control.

This family of three was indeed interesting. The student's mother seemed completely unaware of the situation, while the father seemed to grasp the seriousness of the matter but still harbored a glimmer of hope. From his eyes and movements, I could tell he did not really think a single online post could do much harm, but he also understood that we had absolute control over his child. In his mind, he was likely weighing the pros and cons of various actions—should he resist to the end, try to argue his way out, or completely submit? As for the student himself, his eyes first showed confusion, then shifted to resentment, followed by disdain, and finally transformed into fear. These four emotions seemed to be blended together in a mixer, undergoing a chemical reaction until they became one.

In truth, I, like the student's father, was considering the next steps, much as I had once considered my son's future. But they had already made up their minds and would not allow me to waver. She stood behind me, patted my shoulder, and then walked in front of me. She said, "We are all civilized people; we will use reason to persuade the other side and then present a fair negotiating condition." There was a light in her eyes that I had never seen before—this light reminded me again of today's sunshine—it had the courage to defeat darkness, the ruthlessness to scorch the earth, the joy of a child receiving a reward, and the relief of a silkworm breaking out of its cocoon. Her eyes seemed to be telling me that the time had come for the next step. So, I produced the evidence of the student's guilt. Eagerly, I unfolded the paper, waving it in front of the student's father. The scent of ink from the paper reminded me of the snacks I had eaten as a child; the newspapers wrapped around those snacks always gave off a strange but addictive aroma—whenever I smelled it, I knew I would have a happy and wonderful day.

I was not the only one impatient—the student was impatient to reject our calling the stack of papers evidence, his mother was impatient to plead with us, and his father was impatiently considering his next move. She, too, began to grow anxious. She shone the light in her eyes on others; my brother responded with the same look, and others began to take action. My brother found his favorite good wine, the others found gold jewelry, and she found a famous painting. These were all solid pieces of evidence: the top-grade wine suggested that the student's father lived a leisurely and comfortable life; the gold jewelry implied that the student's mother had a blessed marriage; and the painting suggested that this family had an unusual sense of taste. These three objects seemed ordinary, but combined with the student's mockery of me, they were no longer ordinary—living a comfortable life was the reason the student looked down on the school, because if life were difficult, no one would care whether the school's buildings leaked; a blessed marriage meant a happy family, and a happy family meant that the parents and children were on the same side, which could even mean that the student's parents were also against us; finally, if the whole family had enough artistic taste to appreciate a painting, then it was only natural that the student would pay attention to details, which is why he noticed problems with the school's building quality.

Of course, these were her and my thoughts. In my brother's eyes, good wine, gold jewelry, and famous paintings all indicated a wealth greater than that of ordinary people. I understood that, as an officer, he could not tolerate any of this—he instinctively saw young people as his soldiers, and a soldier should not have what only officers were entitled to. But what he could not tolerate even more was that a child, or rather an ordinary foot soldier, dared to prevent him from drinking. This was an insult he had never endured; even when his soldiers gnawed on hard, cold buns, none dared to complain about him eating meat and drinking wine. My brother picked up a bottle of alcohol and smashed it on the floor, and the aroma instantly filled the entire room. This did reassure me somewhat—people need to vent; venting always brings a bit more tolerance. But his anger had not completely dissipated, and things seemed to have gone beyond what I had initially expected—I hadn't thought that a seventeen- or eighteen-year-old could truly be so fearless. When I told him that "spreading rumors can lead to the death penalty," his expression actually relaxed, and this statement seemed to add to his anger, as if he were hoping for a chance to sacrifice his life for a cause or simply considered my threat a joke.

I thought that perhaps I had failed: I had bet that he did not understand the law, and that fear would make him submit, while he bet that I did not dare enforce the "law." Even though I confidently assured him that rumor-spreading could indeed lead to the death penalty, that this was determined by the international situation, that if everyone spread rumors, there would be no hope for the nation, no hope for the people, and the ultimate result would be our total defeat in our struggle against the world—a defeat of the most devastating kind. All of us added to my statement with our own comments—every one of us blurred the line between child and adult; perhaps there was never any line to begin with. No one treats another person more leniently, especially when that person takes on the role of an enemy; when someone becomes an enemy, no one cares whether they are right or wrong; all they care about is winning or losing in the end.

We all understood this principle, so she and my brothers searched more diligently for possible evidence of the student's crime in his home; it did not really matter whether this evidence proved he spread rumors. As long as it showed that he or his parents had flaws in their morality or behavior, we would be one step closer to victory. The student tried to stop us, but he did not order us to stop with words; instead, he attempted to block our advance with his body—this was also evidence of his guilt. At this moment, I began to understand my brother. He had once said that soldiers who do not obey their superiors are never good soldiers; they will betray their party and country, shamelessly selling their compatriots and even the nation to the enemy. I could foresee how a professional soldier would deal with a recalcitrant enemy, and I could also feel the fury a group of professional teachers might have toward a stubborn student. At this moment, I admired my own calmness; the student's hostility had been directed at me, so I should have been the one most enraged, but my brothers seemed angrier than I was. In this battle, there seemed to be no distinction between offense and defense—both sides were attacking; we could only advance, and retreat was not an option.

It was my brother who came up with the way to break the deadlock. He had long ago arranged for the chief of police to issue certificates of mental illness for the student's parents and presented these as our most important bargaining chip. Then, the student truly lost his mind—he, filled with his dissatisfaction, grievance, and anger, launched an attack on four teachers and a regimental commander of the People's Liberation Army. The outcome was predictable: the frail high school student was easily subdued by five grown men, but he continued to get up and attack. Finally, exhausted, the student used the last of his strength to charge at my brother. This brawny soldier could only lift the powerless student and throw him toward the nearest window behind him—it might not have been the perfect solution, but it was the only one. At this point, that certificate was no longer a bargaining chip but a means to protect everything we had—who would believe the testimony of two mentally ill people? If they did not speak of what happened today, they might still have a chance, but if they did, the only end for them would be prison or a life in a psychiatric hospital.

I could see that when my brother countered the student, his emotions matched the student's exactly. He, too, was unwilling, aggrieved, and angry—he was unwilling to accept that a soldier, so honorable as he, would face an attack from a child; he also felt aggrieved for me, because as a principal, a teacher with students all over the country, I had suffered the insult of a high school student; he could not calmly accept that the reputation of our family, loyal for generations, should be sullied and mocked by an unknown junior; his anger was because he saw a trace of rebellion in this student, and as a soldier, he would never allow anyone to defy authority, especially when that authority represented the party and the country.

And so, it all ended. If we only consider the

matter itself, then I was undoubtedly the victor—I preserved my reputation, saved my brothers' livelihoods, and protected her. But at the same time, I also failed—I had no idea that one of her objectives was the painting in the student's house, so I started to mock my own ignorance once more. As for the gold and other valuables my brothers took, they could serve as proof of our nobility, or they could be regarded as spoils of war for my brothers—regardless, they had fought for the school's honor, and more specifically, for me alone. Therefore, I took none of their spoils. However, like most people, I fear death, not because of the corpse itself, but because even a dead person can influence the course of history. I cannot determine what story this body might tell the world or what result that story might bring about.

Afterwards, we organized a dinner. My brother invited his old regiment commander, though we all called him "Chief"—he was the director of the city's police department. The most remarkable part of him was his tongue; when he spoke, it was even more captivating than the kiss of a beautiful woman. A slight tremble of his tongue tip could deliver an acquittal that would grant me a second life. I knew that once I was absolved of responsibility, this matter would be completely behind us; a battle waged for dignity had ended, and naturally, we were the victors. He said it was a tragedy, but merely an accident. Every year, countless students across the city commit suicide due to academic pressure or emotional disputes; this case could be no exception. The most important thing was that we had saved the face of the leaders; for that, we were heroes. At the very moment the chief finished speaking, a peculiar scent filled the private room in the hotel: it was a blend of the rich aroma of fine wine and the savory scent of delicacies, accompanied by an air of relaxation that stimulated the dopamine in everyone's body. I had not experienced this kind of relief in a long time— not even from my wife and child, only from her.

I said to the Chief, "We were forced into this. We are all innocent people. No one wanted to cause trouble for the leaders. I must first confess my own shortcomings in educating students, and then thank the leaders for their care and support."

My brother said to his old commander, "We were 'upholding justice on behalf of heaven'[13]... or rather, we were fighting for the Party and the country. This is purely within our duty. Look at those famous paintings and gold jewelry; who knows how much harm they have done to our motherland? Who knows how many of the artifacts in the British Museum were sold by them, a family of smugglers? And that boy, he cannot possibly be unaware that the provincial leaders have praised our school. If this kind of traitor exists, who knows what terrible things he might do in the future? Fortunately, we won in the end."

She added, "Chief, even if this student hadn't spread rumors online, we still would have had to deal with him. He was also in an early romantic relationship! This time, we have responded to the Party and the country's call to resolutely combat rumor-mongering. We are all heroes, and we are fortunate to have become heroes. This is the mission of our school, and I believe it is also our personal fate. However, after this incident, I must ask our comrades at the Cyberspace Affairs Commission[14] to keep a closer watch on online public opinion."

With that, everyone stood up once more, raised their glasses, and drank the clear liquor in a single gulp. Alcohol is a magical thing. It can be filled with joy or sorrow; it can make people forget many things or bring countless memories rushing back; it has the power to awaken every cell in the body or help people sleep soundly. And so, after a bottle of baijiu was roughly poured into my stomach, I remembered the superficial harmony between my wife, my child, and me today, and I also recalled the warm moments I had once shared with my family. I forgot that she had been with other men in the past, yet I could clearly remember the tender feelings between us when we were together. At that moment, I desperately wanted to spend another beautiful night with her, but drowsiness, uninvited, took over my mind.

So, on the night after the banquet ended, I had another dream. In this dream, her painting came to life: we stood at the bow of the battleship, calmly gazing at the distant sea—my stage. The endless steel behemoths clashed with each other, smoke billowing and rising high into the sky. When everything finally settled down, she pulled a bottle of whiskey, warmed by her body, from her chest; the bottle was still covered in sea salt crystals left behind as seawater evaporated. We shared that bottle of whiskey, celebrating our victory. Then, I awoke suddenly to hear her gentle breathing beside me, while the insects outside the window whispered idly, and the morning sun, as always, slowly peeked out. The scene was so beautiful, so beautiful that it was almost overwhelming.

Breaking Free

I

When I walked out of the awards ceremony hall, a large group of colleagues came up to congratulate me—just like when I first came to this provincial key high school to become an art teacher, receiving reactions from my family members. I could tell that some of them were not genuinely willing to utter words of praise, but their reluctance did not affect my mood. I responded to their congratulations with a sincere yet indifferent attitude, all the while clutching the award certificate tightly to prevent the drizzling rain from defiling this sacred memento. I subconsciously stroked the red fibers on the cover of the certificate with my fingers, trying to recall the contents inside: the colored paper adorned with intricate and beautiful patterns, with a deep embossed seal at the bottom. However, the only regret I felt was that such an exquisite certificate merely mentioned that I had been honored as a "Provincial Model Teacher of Ethics," without specifying what I had done— which, to say the least, was disappointing. I thought, if I hadn't had this certificate in my hand, who would have known the title I had once earned? And even if others had known, how would they have known why I had won the award?

After the awards ceremony, I went straight home. As usual, I opened the door, took off my muddy shoes, changed into pajamas, and sat at my desk, gazing at my award certificate. In an instant, my previous regret vanished—I saw my name on the certificate and thought that from now on, this honor would be tightly bound to my name. I realized that what I had specifically done no longer mattered; what mattered was what I had received—a lesson every teacher understands. Each important stage of life is like answering a multiple-choice or fill-in-the-blank question. Even if the answer is guessed correctly by sheer luck, as long as it is correct, one receives full marks; conversely, even if a wrong answer comes from careful calculation, it is still wrong, and the answerer will lose all points, potentially losing the chance to attend university, perhaps even becoming a failure in the eyes of society.

Gradually, it grew darker outside. I cooked some rice, reheated the leftovers from the previous day in the microwave, and thus resolved my dinner. Today, I seemed unconcerned about food and drink, for such meals would not always stay with me; but honor was different—today, it emitted a rich fragrance that whetted my appetite, and I firmly believed it would continue to exist from today onward, until the last person who remembered me died. I told myself, this is the value of honor; if it could truly be remembered for that long, it would be worth coming to this world. However, as this

thought surfaced, the regret I had just cast aside
took off its disguise—it said that others only
remembered the title on the certificate; this title was
never the answer to any fill-in-the-blank question
but merely the score written in the top right corner
of an essay exam, devoid of content.

Thus, my thoughts tangled and circled until I
felt a trace of drowsiness. I slowly placed the bowls
and chopsticks into the sink, intending to wash them
the next day, and then undressed, stepped into the
shower, and set the water temperature high. I liked
watching the stream of water from the showerhead
while bathing—I would gaze at the mist created by
the hot water, watching myself being slowly
enveloped, as if I had ascended into the clouds,
looking down on all my past memories. This was a
good time for self-examination—bathing was like
an open-book exam, my memories the textbook,
and the questions I asked myself were the test
questions.

"Was this honor earned by chance or
inevitability?"

The first question stumped me. I initially
answered myself that it was by chance since not
every teacher could achieve such an illustrious
honor. Then, I corrected myself—I said it was
inevitable—at least, it should be inevitable for me. I
saved a student's life; should not I deserve a
provincial honor for that? Whether it was my long-

term work or that instinctive reaction at that moment, both destined that I should be praised.

Then, I asked myself a second question, "Is it too simple to earn such an honor for just doing one thing?"

Indeed, it seemed not difficult at all, almost easy: I pushed a student away from an oncoming car, allowing him to live happily ever after, and that was all. Although the citation only mentioned this specific example, it was not limited to praising me for saving a student's life. The host, with a sweet voice, described me as not only a lifesaver in that moment but also a subject leader and a mentor of the students' souls, a navigator on their journey of life. On stage, I recited my well-prepared lines, stating that my teaching philosophy was "shaping the future with love," my goal was "cultivating talents for the Party and the country," and my approach was "influencing people with a noble character, treating them with kindness, guiding them with profound knowledge, and protecting them with a broad mind." It seemed that people only enjoyed such vague descriptions, allowing their imagination to run wild—their state in the grand hall was essentially no different from mine here in the shower. The applause and words from the awards ceremony echoed in my ears, prompting me to ask myself why I had received an award for "teaching ethics" rather than for "heroic bravery."

I closed the shower while pondering this, grabbed a towel from the nearby rack, and dried myself. My body, affected by the hot water, felt somewhat fatigued, so I went straight to the bedroom and lay down on the bed. At the moment my back touched the mattress, I suddenly realized the answer to my earlier question: "Heroic bravery" evaluates a single event, like a point, while "Model Teacher of Ethics" offers an overall assessment, like a line. And when did this line—or my path— actually begin?

This question tortured me for ten minutes. I thought, forget it, and do not dwell on this; I have work tomorrow. So I removed the hairpin from my long hair and casually tossed it onto the wooden bedside table. But the sound of the hairpin hitting the table was like a bullet shattering my thoughts—I suddenly realized that my path began with a hairpin. When this thought emerged, it was as if an electric current ran through my tired muscles; the current started from my toes, pierced through every organ in my body, and reached the top of my head. I was suddenly wide awake, so I got out of bed, went to the wardrobe, and retrieved another hairpin from a corner on the top shelf.

It was a red hairpin encrusted with rhinestones. I had kept it in that corner of the wardrobe for many years, to the point that the rhinestones had taken on a faint yellow hue. Yet, its outdated style and prominent signs of fading convinced me that it had witnessed my history. When I held it in my palm, it seemed to still emit a faint warmth. I knew this hairpin was just a small item made from the most ordinary plastic and paint, but under the right light, it could still radiate a dazzling glow. It held my hand and forcibly dragged me back many years— back then, I was already a teacher with two years of experience. I do not know whether to call myself an "old teacher" at that time, but at least I could confidently teach my students, though two years was not a long time. I still remember that I loved listening to the experienced teachers share their insights. An older teacher once told me that to be a successful teacher, teaching is secondary, and the students' grades are even less important. The most important thing is to maintain good relations with the students' parents; as long as the parents approve, the students' opinions are not that important and not worth the teacher's attention.

I looked at her, puzzled. She smiled, seemingly guessing what I was thinking, and took a sip of cold tea from her cup, then said that the tuition fees are paid by the parents, it's the parents who decide whether to enroll their children in extra classes, and it's the parents who spread the teacher's reputation by word of mouth, which has nothing to do with the students. She did not elaborate further, nor did she teach me what exactly I should do. Like a forest ranger trying to predict the weather by watching the clouds, I searched for the path forward in her few words. I thought this confusion would always accompany me, but one night, a light appeared on the road—after finishing a parents' meeting, I walked into the office, exhausted, sat heavily in the cold, hard wooden chair, and began to organize my briefcase. At that moment, a mother pushed open the office door. I suppressed my desire to go home and earnestly told her about the strengths of her child in both learning and life and areas that needed improvement. I looked into her eyes and calmly expressed my thoughts, and she nodded thoughtfully at times and smiled slightly at others. She calmly accepted everything I said.

I thought, maybe this was what the older teacher meant by "maintaining a good relationship with the parents"—our conversation was very pleasant, almost not like one between a teacher and a student's parent. But when the teachings of the older teacher echoed in my mind, I told myself this was not enough. The harmony I had just felt suddenly vanished, replaced by my urgency and the parent's cautiousness—I suddenly realized that the previous harmony was just a superficial illusion, so it did not set me apart from other ordinary teachers, nor did it change the nature of our relationship. The only way to become friends with the parents was through casual conversation. I suppressed my urgency and did everything I could to make the transition more natural. So, I said to this elegant mother:

"Hey, your hairpin looks nice. Where did you get it?"

The moment I said this, I noticed I paused for half a second, suddenly regretting my rashness. However, the parent did not seem bothered by my abruptness. She quickly smiled, lowered her head slightly, and took off the hairpin, then handed it to me. I instinctively uttered words of refusal, but my hands, afraid the hairpin would fall to the ground, reached out and caught it. I was sure I accepted the hairpin not because I wanted such a cheap plastic trinket—just like when I was young and refused the New Year's red envelopes[15] from my relatives while firmly holding them in my hand. Following my parents' teachings, I would resolutely refuse the envelopes, but I always knew that whether I refused or not, the envelopes would ultimately be mine. So, I persisted in refusing, even though I had never successfully refused once. And thus, I became the new owner of this hairpin. The parent seemed delighted, perhaps because I accepted her, or perhaps because my image in her mind was no longer that of a lofty teacher but a friend.

Reflecting back to this point, I carefully placed the hairpin back in its original spot. I had never imagined that a small hairpin could completely change my mindset. I used to enjoy sleeping in on leisurely weekends; the curtains would block the midday sun from entering my room, helping me fulfill this simple dream. Often, after waking up naturally, I would first recall what I had done throughout the past week. Once I finished this mental recap, I would reach for my phone on the bedside table, using it to find my way out of bed and muster the courage to face the start of a new day. Before I acquired this hairpin, my thoughts were mostly filled with busy work and endless political studies. But after I got it, I began to feel a sense of satisfaction in being a teacher.

However, today, when I closed the wardrobe door, I finally understood why I felt this satisfaction—I seemed to have grasped the meaning behind the words of the older teacher and realized why, although we were all earning similar salaries, she could live so comfortably. The reason was not because she "remained indifferent to fame and fortune, and found peace in quiet," nor because she "neither rejoiced over things nor grieved over herself." Instead, this hairpin had subtly planted a belief deep in my subconscious: being a teacher could allow one to easily build relationships with others, and having such connections could, in turn, bring substantial benefits.

The word "benefit" might sound too vast and tainted, but the reason I called such a cheap hairpin a "benefit" was because I saw the great potential hidden behind it. When I accepted this hairpin, the word "benefit" flashed through my mind, though at that time, I did not understand why I thought so, attributing it to my fatigue-induced ramblings. After the parent turned and left my office, I dismissed my earlier thought. I told myself that it was just a fleeting notion; since the first day I became a teacher, the only "benefit" I had expected was my salary. My parents had advised me that, as a girl, finding a stable job was good enough, especially being a teacher—a simple work environment, and it would be easy to get married.

I believed this flimsy advice, not because my parents' words had any inherent persuasiveness, but due to my own inherent laziness. Many people may have grand ambitions but eventually realize that life is nothing more than basic necessities, and everything else is unimportant. Then, those unimportant things are slowly forgotten. I am an example of this—perhaps I once boasted in elementary school that I wanted to be both a painter and a scientist, or maybe in middle school, I had the delusion of being admitted to Tsinghua or Peking University. But when I realized that these dreams were unrealistic, they disappeared without a trace, never to resurface; then, more practical dreams occupied my mind entirely.

Gradually, my dream became to do my job

well and to teach my students properly. To put it more grandiosely, it was to help others succeed. For a time, I believed that the students' grades on their exam papers were everything—those red numbers were not just the students' scores, but my medals. In my vision, when students achieved good grades, they would go to good universities, find good jobs, and eventually be grateful for the help I, as their teacher, had given them. They might even help me in some coincidental moment in the future. I regarded their future gratitude as "benefit" beyond my salary—something that seemed hard to convert into specific monetary value; and even if it could be monetized, it would require patience and luck.

A history teacher in my office once heard me discussing my ideas. Later, like a mentor, he taught me that my thoughts were only half right. He said my thinking focused solely on "teaching" but completely neglected "educating." Gaining knowledge is certainly important, but beyond the college entrance exams, where else would this knowledge appear? Its ultimate value is nothing more than being graded on an exam paper; beyond that, it is useless. No one needs to apply biological knowledge when seeking medical treatment; they just need a prescription from a doctor. No one needs plane geometry or classical Chinese rhetoric. The art of "educating," he explained, lies in us teachers imparting the skills students will need to survive in society.

I did not continue to ask how one should "educate." I knew that if I rashly asked that question, he would not be able to provide a specific answer on how to do it; even if he did answer, I would still need to ponder every word he said on my own. We had grown accustomed to immersing ourselves in grand narratives, never attempting to make them concrete. But the history teacher's words were a wake-up call for me—so I no longer considered myself an experienced teacher but rather a novice who had never ventured into society. I began paying attention to how the genuinely accomplished veteran teachers educated their students, even preparing a notebook to meticulously document all their efforts for their careers. Recalling this, I was already lying in bed. I wrapped myself tightly in the quilt, as if it were a shroud— inside were my memories, fixed by time, while outside was the ever-changing present. In my memories, there was always something in the words I had recorded that puzzled me. They first settled, then rotted, and finally dried up like a blood-drained carcass—long dead, yet still lifelike.

The history teacher imparted his experience to me in the office; we were five teachers chatting together when he summarized his insights. Every detail from that time was etched into my memory. The moment he demonstrated to me happened in the office as well—one day, he asked me, "What's the name of that kid in your class who is going to study in the U.S.?" His gaze had never looked so furious—there seemed to be a great fire in his eyes, devouring everything around. Though his anger was not directed at me, I felt an unprecedented fear. I asked him what had happened, and he first earnestly told me that this was the right moment for "educating," then lit the cigarette in his hand, slowly inhaled and exhaled, seemingly unwilling to tell me what had specifically occurred.

The white smoke blurred my vision. Perhaps he saw I was reluctant to leave, or perhaps because I was still hesitating to tell him the student's name, he seemed to make a decision in an instant. He told me he had worked hard teaching the students, but the student and his parents were ungrateful, completely disregarding him, the history teacher. I was even more puzzled, and unconsciously, my confusion was written all over my face. Only then did he tell me that the student had asked the school for a proof of enrollment but did not know that he was in charge of the academic affairs office, nor had he given him even a penny as a bribe. I said nothing— not a word. At that time, I did not know how to respond, but I considered many possibilities: if I said the student had not given me a bribe either, the history teacher might draw me into his side. But if I lied and said I had received a bribe, I might become a target for everyone.

Fortunately, he did not give me a chance to speak. He continued to paint vivid scenarios of the student being ostracized, shot, or even betraying his country and murdering his compatriots in America. But the jealousy and displeasure in his expression did not dissipate with his venting; on the contrary, his emotions seemed to be approaching the brink of explosion. His lips grew increasingly dry, and the beads of sweat on his forehead glistened and trickled down his cheeks, yet he had no intention of quenching his thirst with the cold tea on the table. Where did his anger, even hatred, come from? I thought it must be jealousy. Jealousy is an emotion that can be found everywhere; it exists, but its existence is built upon fiction and imagination. Initially, I felt that the decisions made by the student and the parents had nothing to do with me, and I had no right to interfere. However, when I figured this out, his reaction started to make sense—in his imagination, the student, with wealthy parents, squandered money abroad in a life of debauchery and ultimately harmed his own country for sordid purposes. Regardless of whether this imagination was reasonable, as long as there was the slightest possibility, in the world he had constructed, this seemingly fictional scenario would inevitably come to pass.

When the other teachers followed the bell's

call to their classrooms, only the history teacher and I remained in the office. The bell seemed to have a calming effect on every living being in the school, and he was no exception. With a slightly trembling right hand, he took a cigarette pack from his jacket pocket, fumbled for a lighter from his pants pocket, and held the cigarette in his mouth with a twisted expression. After taking a puff, his tone abandoned the passionate emotion from earlier, becoming steady and profound—he once again became the elder mentor who had patiently guided me. He said:

"Apart from teaching lessons, imparting the principles of human interaction to students is also part of my 'educational' work. Students must learn gratitude and, more importantly, how to read people and situations—this is the most important lesson in their lives, more important than any knowledge they might learn. Young people who cannot read people and situations will suffer greatly in the future. Sometimes, I also reflect on whether it's the case that history lessons are not important and that history teachers are not valued, or if there's something wrong with my approach. I've told the students many times, 'Your Chinese teacher likes antiques and paintings, the English teacher likes cosmetics, the math teacher likes Jin Jun Mei and Da Hong Pao tea[16], and as for me, just a token will do.' But how many of them have listened? If they cannot even manage a small gesture, how will they fare in society? I ask them to do this for their own good. Sadly, not only do the students not appreciate it, but the parents also do not teach their children."

That night, when I got home, I could not help but continue to recall every scene that had unfolded during the day. I suddenly realized that the jealousy displayed in front of others is actually a privilege reserved for those in power, not the other way around. Those in lower positions might feel jealous of those above them, but they rarely dare, or are able, to take any real action. On the contrary, when someone who has always been humble surpasses a person in power in some way, the person in power will instinctively retaliate. However, what he said about "educating people" did have some truth, even a lot of sense—children will eventually face society, and the authority figures they encounter there will be far more ruthless than those in school. I told myself that if making children experience cruelty in advance could prepare them for it, then why not consider it a form of kindness?

Later, this notion not only became one of my guiding principles for educating students but also served as the preamble to my self-reflection. This transformation took time, and the reason I began to change was because I figured out why we wanted children to experience cruelty—it all came down to the word "conformity." Children must experience cruelty simply because others have experienced it; a person who has not experienced it is unfit to integrate into this cruel world. Originally, I thought that the words "conformity" and "non-conformity" carried no difference in praise or blame—they were just two ways of living that did not interfere with each other, a natural outcome of divergent evolution, and an inconsequential personal choice. But then, in a flash, I suddenly realized that I had not received any honors or awards in the first three years of my career, and I recalled the sneers of a colleague when I politely declined a large cash gift from a student's parent. At that moment, I woke up—I had failed simply because I did not conform. It turned out that such seemingly trivial concepts could lead to a total defeat in my competition with others.

At that time, I complained in my heart that all the conflicts and collaborations in the world, whether fights or partnerships, were fundamentally about interests. In the eyes of those who conform, non-conformity implies arrogance, and arrogance suggests hidden aggressiveness; aggressiveness means I might launch an attack against them at any time, potentially harming their interests. Their countermeasures were also simple: isolate themselves from those who do not conform or preemptively show aggression to their imagined enemies—one method being defense, the other offense. The history teacher, with the tone of someone who had been through it all, told me: "If you are too embarrassed to accept gifts, those who do will see you as being aloof. 'Aloof' is not a compliment. When you are aloof, it makes others look bad; in the end, you'll be the one who suffers—reputation, honor, and even wealth will all be beyond your reach."

I did not know whether what he said was simple or profound; I understood every word he spoke, but when I tried to connect his words, countless questions sprouted in my mind. When did "aloofness" become a derogatory term? How does "aloofness" harm the interests of bystanders? Or rather, what exactly are interests? Since then, I've been trying to answer these questions for myself, but to this day, I still haven't found a clear answer.

II

Since I was a child, my interest in painting drove me to learn it, and now painting is my profession. To me, the art contained in a painting is far more profound and mysterious than any other form of art, while also being more approachable. Even now, I still keep every one of my works, even the doodles I created when I first picked up a paintbrush. Through these paintings, I can recall certain details from the process of creation: What my mood was at that time, what I was thinking about, and what sparked the inspiration for that piece.

Thus, every painting of mine is like a mirror casually placed on a street corner—the images reflected in this mirror are always real and random; these images have no opinion, no stance, and no logic. They are impossible to interpret, and often lack any meaning. Sometimes, I might stop my brush due to an inadvertent mistake, while in another painting, the same mistake might create a stunning effect. These spontaneous, unrestrained images are what constitute the world. At moments like this, everything in the world forms a tenuous connection with one another, like the fleeting exchange of glances between strangers on opposite sides of a street, or the inadvertent interaction between the distant sun and the fish in a stream. So, when I sense the connection between all things in my uneven works, I emerged from years of confusion—it turned out that everything happening to me, though random, was also real, and all things were interconnected; therefore, everything was also inevitable. This realization signifies that I have stopped obsessing over defying fate or that, at some point, I realized I am merely a person who goes with the flow—if something happens, it is something that was meant to happen. As an observer and an ordinary person struggling to survive, I can only let it happen; at the same time, if I want to continue living, I must calmly accept everything that happens around me.

So, I calmly accepted the certificate from the State Department of Education, accepted the fact that I had become a hero, and even accepted those things that overturned my understanding, including death—I know life and death are fated, but I also believe that death has nothing to do with me for the time being. However, when I see others able to look past life and death, I add this term to my personal dictionary; like the flawed sketch I created when I was ten years old, its arrival was not something I intended but rather some irresistible force of fate. When I was younger, I would cry bitterly over such a small mistake, but as I grew older, I became indifferent to such trivial matters.

However, when I became indifferent, I started

to find it hard to understand those who could not. For example, my colleague sitting next to me—she is the homeroom teacher of a humanities class and the head of the school's moral education department. When she found out that our school's average score in the joint exam was tied for first place in the state with another school, she first smiled, then picked up her phone to check something, sometimes beaming with joy and sometimes scowling with anger. She touched her wedding ring, took a sip from her cup, and then looked up at a small spider wandering across the ceiling, sighing deeply. She pressed her hands on the table and stood up, the sound of her high heels clacking on the floor as she left the office. I could not help but glance at the other teachers in the office; everyone seemed indifferent to the news, as if the students' scores had nothing to do with them. At that time, I could not understand why an adult could have such intense emotional swings. To her, this insignificant score seemed like a matter of utmost importance. Early in my childhood, I had learned to suppress such emotions; I had once told myself that baseless emotions were a big taboo in creation and perhaps also a major taboo in life. To put it nicely, it's called "being a person of feeling," but to put it bluntly, it's just "being capricious."

But later, I realized that changeable emotions are not necessarily harmful, at least not to everyone.

Her emotions guided her actions. So she followed through—in her piercing voice, she declared that the person to blame for our school not getting the top spot in the state was a girl. Because of her careless mistake on one question, she only scored 145 in math[17], and thus, our school failed to achieve first place in the state. She said that this mistake was a stain on our school's glorious history, which had caused more than a thousand students in her grade to miss out on sharing the title of state first place.

We listened to her impassioned speech in silence from behind a wall. Everyone knew that, as a state key high school, our school's performance had always been among the best in the state, so much so that we could have started celebrating even before the results were officially released. But the question was, who would feel proud or anxious over an event that kept repeating itself? People feel exhilarated reading about ancient figures who dominated the battlefield, simply because those times are long gone and will never return; all the facts and rumors will never cause any more ripples. Otherwise, no one would want to endure the absurd heat of passion for "white bones exposed in the wild, not a rooster crows for miles" or be willing to become the knife fodder of various warlords.

So, if today someone were still to wail and beat their chest over Liu Bei's defeat at Yiling[18], it could only be for the sake of performance, to conceal some unspeakable motive. All I knew was that this teacher was not raging for the sake of the school's honor, but the experienced teachers' inadvertent sneers seemed to make her purpose abundantly clear. So, how should this girl, who made a mistake on a test, atone for her error? "I am sorry" is a cheap phrase, but when repeated endlessly, it seems to demonstrate sincerity—so the teacher ordered her to apologize once a day to each of the fourteen classes in her grade for thirty days, repenting for her mistake.

And so, the girl repented. She repented so deeply that she became convinced of her own guilt. Three days later, like a leaf, she twirled down from the fifth floor of the school. She was not just like a leaf—she was a leaf, making a slight sound as she hit the ground, and no one cared about her posture as she fell; only the red stain spreading slowly on the cement caught people's attention for a brief moment.

Naturally, my eyes were drawn to it. At that moment, a thought occurred to me: That scene might forever remain in my memory, just as her soul could never leave her classroom. I told myself countless times that if something like this happened again, I should resist my pathetic and ridiculous curiosity, especially regarding those events destined to occur—when this naive girl made a mistake on a test, she was doomed not to survive. I felt wronged for myself, for the participant bore no psychological burden, while I, as an observer, had to bury fear and disgust deep within; I thought, if there were a medicine that could make me forget that scene, I would buy it and swallow it greedily.

Unfortunately, no such medicine exists, but I happened to see another kind at a street pharmacy—cordyceps[19]. This immediately raised a question: Why do humans fear a human corpse but not feel the same way about the corpse of cordyceps? The ultimate fate of a small worm may be to be sun-dried into a mummy, turned to dust in a human mouth, or ground into powder by a roaring machine and dissolved in boiling water. I wondered why the fate of a poor little worm, attached to fungi and living a zombie-like existence in a place without light, does not elicit human sympathy. Soon, I figured out why: No matter how grave the misdeeds, even when it involves life and death, the psychological burden comes only from fear of punishment. People then tell themselves that only life and death are inevitable, and accelerating death is not a crime; on the contrary, it may help the dead escape suffering. Like those vividly displayed cordyceps on the counter, their lives are taken by fungal mycelia, dried by the sun, and crushed by machines, all unrelated to the observing humans; their fate might be due to their lack of hands to wipe the fungi from their foreheads or their lack of intelligence and strength to escape or resist human capture—in people's habitual thinking, such a fate is deemed "destiny" for a small life.

Indeed, everyone has their destiny: The student's death was destiny, my witnessing it was destiny, and even a lifeless place like the "school" has its destiny—it could boast glorious achievements, or it could openly display its bloody, violent side to everyone. If someone asked me if I cared about the student's life or death, I suppose I might hesitate for a moment before answering, "Yes, I do." This hypothetical scenario made me realize that I do not care, because I am not the corpse lying on the concrete ground; what I truly care about is only what others think of me, nothing more. So, what would someone do if they did not care about others' opinions? They might hold a banner with black characters on a white background and cry at the school gate, ignoring the indifferent gazes of passersby and their hurried backs, endlessly muttering to themselves, and then stubbornly resisting the police's handcuffs[20] with anger and defiance—my attitude is my destiny, and their choices are their destiny, too. Even if this event were to happen a hundred times, the process and result would not change because it is the only thing that would ever happen; there is no other possibility.

The process of recollection is like being placed on an autopsy table on a cold night, forcing me to carefully examine my own heart while struggling to resist the scalpel cutting me open—humans are truly contradictory creatures. Only after dissecting myself did I realize that everyone wishes for all things to submit to their feet, but when that moment truly arrives, they begin to doubt the loyalty of all things. The students' oaths to respect their teachers had not yet dissipated from the air when the teachers, as rulers, began to worry that a single death might force the masses beneath them to stop kneeling; meanwhile, those who were kneeling seemed even more afraid of the rulers' suspicion and thus hurriedly offered their tributes. Just a week later, not only had the school returned to calm, but the teachers' office was also piled with various gifts. She, with her seven-month-pregnant belly, opened one package after another in an extremely awkward posture, showing them off to us:

"Look, baby clothes... I do not know if it's a boy or girl, so if they got it wrong, I'll sell them online... Oh, these supplements are nice; I've heard of this brand, it's imported. The supermarket gift cards are okay, but I've got a pile at home I haven't used yet. Flowers are the most pointless, cannot eat them, cannot wear them, and cannot even exchange them for money."

As she rummaged through each gift, she

muttered to herself incessantly. She pulled out a thank-you note from the bouquet, tore it open, glanced at it carelessly, and then casually tossed it into the nearby trash can. Following the arc of the discarded note, my gaze fell upon the overflowing trash bin, and I had to admit that I was beginning to feel a tinge of envy for her. She noticed the envy in my eyes and called my name, then generously offered me a box of pecan nuts, saying she did not like nuts. I did not mind her attitude; I returned to my seat and carefully opened the nut package with scissors. A fragrance I had never smelled before filled my nostrils—it was not that I had never eaten pecans before, but perhaps my brain was telling me through my sense of smell that this was not a box of snacks worth a hundred yuan but something exchanged for a human life; maybe this unique aroma was the original scent of the nuts mixed with a hint of blood. Watching her devour Danish cookies and Belgian chocolates, I suddenly realized that even among teachers, there could be such a vast difference—while I could let go of minor issues, accept that I might never become a billionaire, and face the reality of never receiving gifts from parents, others might not be so easily reconciled.

I am not interested in bloodshed, but having been a teacher for so many years, I have come to understand one thing: For one person to succeed, another—or even a group of people—must make sacrifices. Just like for someone to come first, there must be someone at the bottom. This sacrifice can be spiritual, material, or even physical. When someone is useless in a particular context, being sacrificed becomes an expected outcome—a poor student is like a weightlifter without arms; no one will accept their existence anymore. It was through this slaughter that I understood: A person's existence itself holds no meaning—only existence that is recognized and proven meaningful is true existence.

I believe my existence now has meaning, and this certificate of honor is proof of that. So, when did I start existing? I answered myself without hesitation: I started existing the moment I was recognized. When the school decided to establish a Master Teacher Studio named after me, I told myself that I had been recognized. At that moment, I hadn't yet realized that this was the point when I officially existed in this world.

Recognition comes from others, but the recognition of others is based on one's actions—I clearly remember the day before I was recognized. It was a night of torrential rain. At the end of the workday, as soon as I stepped out of the teaching building, my shoes were filled with water, yet I had no choice but to hold up a flimsy umbrella as I walked toward the bus stop. The streetlights, with their dim yellow glow, illuminated the heavy raindrops and occasionally flickering purple or pink lights along the roadside. I kept complaining about the gusty wind accompanying the rain, tilting my umbrella against the direction of the wind to shield my face from the water droplets. I passed countless "Beauty and Hair" shops with strange lighting. Normally, I would have been used to their presence, but this day was different—another art teacher from the school stood at the door, looking around, before being led inside by a girl in a low-cut dress.

How old was that girl? Maybe sixteen, maybe eighteen, but that did not matter. What mattered was that the school was planning to set up an Art Master Teacher Studio, and its leader could either be me or him. I stood on the side of the road, letting the rain soak my shoes and pants. Trembling and hesitant, I finally struggled to pull out my phone and dialed the police. I walked across the street through the puddles, silently watching the police car arrive with its flashing red and blue lights[21]. Perhaps he had already ended his night of pleasure, or maybe he had just finished bathing with the girl, but either way, at the moment the police arrived, he was no longer recognized and had lost his reason for existence. The meaning that had once been attached to his name was instantly transferred to me. At that moment, he was like a bird singing loudly on a branch just a moment before; the moment the gunshot rang out, only its body remained in the world. Its previous song would be forgotten, its colorful feathers plucked, and the only thing left for it was to accept its fate—to be sprinkled with seasoning by humans, consumed with alcohol, and finally turned into a topic of conversation at the dining table.

Thus, competition is the only interpersonal relationship in the school. "Mutualism" is a concept that only appears in biology textbooks, and "helping each other" frequently shows up in essay collections, class speeches, or student award materials but never in reality. Textbooks repeatedly emphasize the survival rules of mutual benefit, but everyone knows that helping others will not provide any sense of accomplishment. The reason this concept appears in textbooks is only because mutual benefit is a skill that needs to be learned, unlike eating or drinking, which are inherent instincts—textbooks never teach us how to eat or drink.

We teachers understand this principle even better. A student's grades, high or low, do not affect our income or reputation, so achieving our satisfaction is the correct answer to every question in our personal lives. I am very fortunate to have realized this; otherwise, no matter how many years passed, I would have remained a failure who worked hard but never gained honor or wealth. If there had been a path where you could see the end at a glance, that path would certainly not have led to success. The reason is simple: if following the rules led to success, then everyone would keep progressing on a fixed path, and life would have no ups and downs. But the harsh reality is the exact opposite—without the experience of struggling in the dark, there can be no success. So, I started reflecting on those countless nights when I tossed and turned over students' grades. At that moment, I could not help but laugh at my own childishness; then I became serious again and warned myself to change the status quo, especially since the road ahead was not as dark as I had imagined—at least I could still learn from the experiences of others.

As I recalled this, I clearly felt my heart race. It was like a heavy hammer striking every inch of my muscles, telling me that this was what "thrilled" felt like. If my brain and heart were separate, they would surely be arguing: The brain would say, "It's time to sleep," while the heart would say, "Pleasure and enjoyment are today's themes." I thought the heart was right—pleasure should not only be today's theme but also the theme of life. My eyes had adjusted to the darkness in the room, so I opened them and stared at the patterns on the wallpaper on the ceiling, trying to find some order in the chaos, like counting sheep in my mind to coax myself to sleep. But these chaotic patterns seemed exactly like my life—no beginning, no end, just a tangle of lines with no apparent order, much like how I cannot remember when my daughter started growing distant from me or when the long, drawn-out cold war with my husband began. I told myself that there was no point in dwelling on these sad things, that the die was cast. But I found I could not convince myself—sad things are like nightmares; they can wake me from all illusions. But happy things seem to have no meaning either; they only keep me awake, for happiness is as fleeting as a passing cloud.

So, when was the last time something happy happened? Besides getting the certificate today, it seems it had been a long time since I felt such unrestrained joy, so long that I could hardly remember. I glanced out at the all-too-familiar scene outside the window and finally recalled that the last time I felt this kind of happiness, the view outside was exactly the same: A few households still had their lights on, and cars occasionally passed under the streetlights. How did humanity evolve from primitive beings into what we are today? When I was in high school, I often asked myself such slightly sci-fi questions. These questions gradually faded with time, but tonight, I remembered it again; I think I now know the answer—everything that happens to humans is based on our savage nature. Humans, as apex predators, have never changed their bloodthirsty and self-serving instincts. It is precisely this nature that drives people to develop techniques and skills that make them comfortable while accelerating the demise of other individuals. Do I have this nature? I dare not deny it; at least, when I saw the blood bloom on the ground, I felt only disgust and fear, not sympathy. Sometimes, I suspected that "sympathy" is a sentiment against human nature—sympathy means feeling pain for suffering we should not experience, bestowing kindness on the unfortunate, and lowering ourselves to accommodate others. But no one wants to endure unnecessary suffering, and no teacher wants to degrade themselves for a student already deemed inferior—hence, we lose the reason for sympathy, and we also lose the courage for it.

I do not know whether my sympathy has gradually diminished over time or if I was born without much of it, but I always vaguely feel that human emotions seem to have a certain limit—as the sensitivity represented by sympathy decreases, the rationality accustomed to weighing pros and cons occupies the mind. Our emotion tells us to understand the lives of others, to consider the pain of the weak, and to sympathize; but the rationality says, "Can you truly sympathize with so many students and colleagues? If you divide your sympathy into a hundred parts, each part will be pathetically small." The emotional half of my personality always gives vague and unrealistic demands, but the guidance from my rational side is always practical. Yet, at this moment, emotion urges me to continue down this path of meaningless thoughts and memories, while reason commands me to sleep immediately—and for this one night, emotion has managed to convince reason.

III

Before dawn, I glanced at the time and imagined that soon the sun would arrive with its dim light, piercing through the thin curtains without any restraint. After a moment's hesitation, I decided to get up and continue working on my painting—a portrait of a neighbor's puppy. I had already sketched out the lines of the entire piece. I studied my draft, intending to silently praise myself for my work, only to realize it looked no different from a photograph. I sighed and said, "My painting is not even as good as a photo."

My daughter had just returned home, though I had no idea where she had been the previous night. She walked past me and heard my self-critique. She shrugged off her backpack, casually tossing it beside the desk, where it landed heavily on the floor. I was already accustomed to the sight of my daughter returning home after having spent the whole night out. I envied others for their harmonious family lives but felt powerless to change my daughter. All I could do was tell myself to accept it, much like enduring the monthly arrival of my period—something that, even if unpleasant, must be silently endured. Perhaps this was the unique path of my life.

Suppressing all emotional fluctuations, I turned back to my work. The difference between painting and photography is that if you want absolute realism, it's best to take a photo in three seconds. If you choose to create, but your work lacks the imaginative elements guided by subjective intent, then the painting loses its meaning. I've always believed that a painting completed only after all the ideas are conceived beforehand will never be perfect—it cannot capture the unfolding of events, nor can it convey the flow of consciousness. In such cases, painting for the artist is no longer an art but an interrogation. In this interrogation, every predetermined idea poses a question, and the artist must respond with their brush, saying no more than necessary to avoid contradictions, but also not less, as no one will accept a story filled with blanks.

"Interrogation... it's everywhere," I thought, recalling the banquet I would attend with the principal that night. I could not help but feel anxious about it. For me, it was another form of interrogation—I would have to face the gazes and remarks of many influential figures and consider how to respond to each seemingly casual comment they made. I mentally rehearsed various questions I might have to answer: How will we handle the ensuing public opinion? How will we explain this to the other students? What if the truth comes out? I kept trying to convince myself that none of this was my responsibility, and I would not need to answer these questions. But then I would start mentally rehearsing every action I would need to take that evening: how to hold the wine glass, how to do my makeup, what to wear... As these questions disrupted my thoughts, I would once again think of the questions I had already rehearsed, going in circles.

As I was lost in thought, the neighbor rang my doorbell. I hurried to the door, rubbing the paint off my hands before opening it. The neighbor greeted me with a smile, saying he wanted to give me a thousand yuan as payment for the painting. I smiled and politely declined, but I also could not turn down such payment. Initially, I had planned to just paint casually, without putting in too much effort, but with the financial incentive, I decided to take this small task seriously. As in human history, where peace comes only with the exchange of interests— whether between individuals, groups, or nations— this truth has remained unchanged since humanity began. I believe this is human nature; while not its entirety, it is the foundation, the logic behind all human behavior.

Suddenly, I felt that facing the banquet was not such a daunting task after all—there would be an exchange of interests among everyone present, so I told myself that today would have a good outcome. I had seen the results of situations without interest exchange—an irreparable disaster for the loser and some form of punishment, however small, for the victor. Thinking about this, I hesitated and put down my brush. The image of my daughter turning away after dropping her backpack continued to linger in my mind. The scenes from that moment kept flashing before my eyes until they completely took over my thoughts, making it impossible for me to concentrate on completing the painting.

I could not understand why I remembered such a distant event so vividly—it had been ten years ago. Logically, I should have discarded these chaotic fragments of memory, but I hadn't. Back then, I was always, consciously or unconsciously, looking for ways to integrate myself into the group, but I could not directly ask any of my colleagues. It was not until a political science colleague invited me to dinner that I first heard a straightforward explanation:

"You need to learn from the experiences of those who came before you. Look at how other teachers usually do it. Embarrass the parents at the parent-teacher meeting, or find a reason to make a student write a self-critique, and make them rewrite it if it's not good enough. Of course, these methods require some technical skill. If you lack experience, you could just move the students who do not bring you gifts to the back row[22]. Make sure to come up with a reason that seems flimsy, like not drinking water but drinking soda, going to the bathroom during recess without permission, being sick and asking for leave, shaking legs in class, shopping on weekends, or playing with their phones at home. Once they bring you something, you move them back. Trust me, in less than two weeks, you'll be living like the best of them."

I asked him, "Why such reasons?"

"You do not need those who lack discernment to believe you; you just need them to fear and obey you. Using these reasons is just to see who dares not to submit to you. Petty people fear authority, not virtue."

I nodded with a questioning look, but he seemed to sense my confusion and added, "The first lesson for a teacher is to establish authority. To what extent, you ask? Well, let's just say, make them fear you so much they will not even dare admit to doing a good deed; and if they do something wrong, even if they're orphans, you should be able to summon their parents to the school to reprimand them."

I still did not quite grasp the logic behind it. I wanted to ask more questions, but perhaps I did not want to expose my ignorance, so I pretended to understand his teachings and said, "Oh, I see. So, which reason do you think is best?"

"Let me think... Go with the weekend shopping reason. It's an easy label to stick on someone. You can say they are living a capitalist lifestyle that's incompatible with socialism. They cannot refute you, and they will not dare to. Of course, I doubt anyone will question the reasons behind your decision."

"But how will I know if the students went shopping on the weekend?"

"You do not need to know. You just need to know which students and parents do not respect you."

"Thank you. Why are you being so detailed with me? Others would not teach me like this."

"Because I love you."

I suddenly felt awkward and unsure of how to react—that day, it had seemed like every event, every word, every action around me was a surprise. I smiled awkwardly, both because of my lack of understanding and because I was not prepared for his confession. So, I grabbed some food and put it in my bowl, thinking that perhaps these morsels could serve as my excuse for silence. Then, I took a sip of beer to wash down the food that served as my excuse. The beer's mild alcohol content had an unexpected effect—it did not knock me out in that humble restaurant, but it did make my thoughts more active. The alcohol integrated scattered emotions and thoughts into serious plans of action and then shattered the plans into fragmented hopes for the future. It turned the jokes that were on the tip of my tongue into indisputable truths and then transformed those truths into anecdotes that might be buried in my memory years later.

And so, I believed my colleague's words and followed his advice. Before entering the classroom, I asked myself, why was I treating a group of students this way? I had never had such complicated emotional motivations; I felt that my subconscious desire to fit in, my pursuit of status, my longing for wealth, and my confusion about life had all contributed to my feelings at that moment. By the time I had figured this out, one of my feet had already stepped into the classroom. I announced my decision to rearrange the students' seats: I would no longer arrange them according to height or academic performance; instead, those who did not buy things would sit in the front, and those who did would sit in the back.

Actually, the politics teacher who gave me advice was wrong. I did not have to wait two weeks; within just two days, the phone calls and gifts from parents came flooding in. I understood they were worried their children might be categorized as those who "go shopping." I could not refuse the parents' compliments, but I still had to face the disdainful looks from my colleagues. Some of them mocked me with their eyes—mocking how I could be satisfied with a hundred-yuan box of snacks. Others glared with jealousy—because it was not a holiday, I was the only one receiving gifts. I completely understood their feelings, and this kind of feeling is the beginning of hostility. I noticed that two conditions are needed for such hostility to arise: No one around me would envy the world's richest man buying a limited-edition luxury car one day, but they would be jealous if I received a box of ordinary snacks today. Similarly, they would not mock a homeless foreigner, but they would mock a colleague's child for doing poorly on a final exam. So, this hostility can only be generated in a relatively closed group; moreover, the person being targeted must be different from the others in some way—either better or worse. But people's internal scales are always precise yet fragile—they can detect the slightest differences between people, but they can also be tipped by the gentlest breeze.

Soon, those who were jealous of me began to mock me openly. One parent came to me and asked why I arranged the seating based on whether or not students shopped over the weekend. I replied that, with exams approaching, the only task for students is to study; this kind of lifestyle is not acceptable. Moreover, it was in response to the Party Central Committee's call to practice a socialist way of life rather than a decadent consumerist, capitalist lifestyle. Immediately, the parent slapped his large hand on my desk, causing all the teachers and students in the office to fall silent. He shouted angrily:

"My son was buying food for me. Do you not

eat?"

As soon as he finished speaking, he noticed the pile of gifts beside my desk, but he did not seem to grasp the purpose behind punishing the "shopping" behavior. Some teachers discreetly left the office, while others kept their heads down, pretending not to be involved. So, the only sound in the office was the parent repeatedly asking, "Do you not eat?" until the politics teacher and the school security guard escorted him out of the office. When the politics teacher returned, drenched in sweat, from the school gate, he commented on the parent:

"Sure enough, not all bad people are stupid, but all stupid people are certainly bad. Stupidity is an original sin."

As he spoke, he glanced at the pile of gifts I had received. This time, I offered him a box of walnut kernels. He opened the box skillfully and sat beside me. He continued, adding that such a foolish person would undoubtedly pay for it. I said nothing and tried to comfort myself by thinking that having something is better than having nothing; after all, I had already gained some benefits and should feel satisfied. But it was clear that my self-comfort was only that—a hollow reassurance. By the afternoon, the parent had found my daughter at her school and threatened her to bring a message to me. That evening, I reported the matter to the principal. The next day, the parent was arrested by the police; on the third day, his child was expelled from school immediately. I still remember my daughter's reaction when she returned home that night: she was trembling, her words slurred, as she relayed bits and pieces of what the parent had said—I roughly understood—that the parent had seen her buying snacks at the school gate, snatched them away, threw them on the ground, and warned her never to eat again, even if it meant starving to death.

In short, the whole incident was a result of a series of coincidences—the politics teacher just happened to give me this advice, the student just happened to shop over the weekend, the student just happened to have a hot-tempered yet foolish father, and the father just happened to run into my daughter. Looking back now, perhaps it was at that moment that the rift between my daughter and me began to grow. No one can change history, but I firmly believe that some people can manipulate it, like the literati of the past who, in their biographies, continually expressed their biases, even mixing in imagined and fictional details. So, I made a failed attempt—I told my daughter that their fight with her mother was for a few pieces of silver, while her mother's fight with them was to support her life, for her future, and for the dignity of our family.

She glanced at me without saying a word, then turned and left, casually tossing her backpack beside the desk. The heavy books crashed to the floor with a deafening cheer. At that time, I thought my daughter was angry, but I did not scold her for throwing her backpack, only maintained an endless silence. Now, thinking back, that action was probably just something my daughter did casually—just like her actions today, so natural. The words of the politics teacher seemed, in a strange way, not to be a curse on a parent, but rather on me. I hated myself for not having listed every possible scenario in detail, for not having prepared more contingency plans.

I thought I was an optimistic person. If it were anyone else, they might have already despaired over the future. Back then, I thought, I had lost face in front of my colleagues, lost respect in front of parents and students, lost authority in front of my daughter—what should I do next? Fortunately, although I had a moment of despair, that feeling quickly vanished because I told myself that when despair arrives, it means nothing could be worse than the current situation; my daughter was still attending school normally, my husband was earning money as usual, and my job and reputation remained intact. What was there to despair about? Perhaps I was merely worried, not in despair—I worried about my daughter's safety, and I was even more concerned about her psychological health.

"If I look on the bright side, what would I see?" I often asked myself this when I calmed down. Maybe this question made me see my longing for a happy life or my desire for power, but at the same time, I realized that if the law does not punish the masses, then desire is innocent. So, when I heard that the hot-headed parent was arrested for being involved in criminal gang-related activities, I immediately told myself that I had gained valuable experience—I had learned how to manage the details in social interactions. More importantly, I understood that power would always be on my side, and for a simple reason: I represented the school's face, the principal's status, social stability, and even the dignity of the Party. But I also understood that if I could not represent the school, the principal, society, and the Party, then neither I nor my daughter would find peace unless I was willing to be ostracized by this collective.

Therefore, when a student used a few photos as evidence to discredit the principal and my group, I began to feel a deep sense of unease—the meaning of my existence was given to me by this school collective, my promotion opportunities were given by the principal, my salary was paid by the Party, and even my family was arranged by my parents. In other words, everything I have now has nothing to do with the students. Then, my unease transformed into an unprecedented sense of responsibility; it told me I must defend everything I had, and even more so, this collective—this group includes me, the role models I learn from, the principal who looks after me, and a place to belong for the next twenty years. No matter how the individuals in this collective treat me, I must rely on it.

So, I told the principal that we must intimidate the students; otherwise, we would be increasingly passive in the future. And we must always have backup plans, always consider every possibility. He agreed and even decided to bring along his soldier-turned-bully brother. I did not like him; there was always a kind of indescribable rage in his eyes, almost a murderous intent. I had a feeling he might cause our plans to fail, but I did not know how to prevent him from getting involved in our affairs. However, on second thought, perhaps we did need such aggression. At this moment, we no longer saw the students as our students, much less as employers who paid us; they were enemies—like soldiers facing off on a battlefield, where a uniform alone could define a person's stance, and that stance would decide where their gun would point to.

Quickly, all the students learned a lesson they would never forget: when beliefs clash, power is the only deciding factor, and victory determines who is right or wrong. No student dared to challenge us anymore, at least not openly accuse us. Even if some students voiced harmless complaints online, their classmates would help suppress those noises:

"Do you have any evidence that it was the

teachers who did it? Any recordings or videos? Liars deserve to die!"

"Do not tell me 'you weren't there, so how would you know.' Even if I was not there, I still know what kind of people my teachers are!"

"Even if the teachers killed someone, I'd still admire them. Without them, I would not be where I am today. Come hit me if you are so tough!"

"Anyone who opposes the teachers will be traitors and lackeys, selling out our country in the future, without exception."

"The teachers have shown you so much kindness, and you use your life to tarnish your mentors. Is that something a human being would do?"

"Even if the teachers did something wrong, you must accept it. 'A teacher for a day, a father for life.' Would you blame your father for criticizing you?"

"I saw it with my own eyes; it was that student who jumped down!"[23]

When these comments appeared before me, it felt like the heavy stone in my heart was slowly settling down. I remembered sitting in the car, ready to leave the neighborhood, feeling a sudden fear; I had never imagined I would witness death again. At that moment, I suddenly realized that once I had defended the school and the principal, I also needed to defend myself—this collective might not stand up for me. To a collective that considers itself superior, protecting an insignificant member would be a demeaning act. Therefore, I needed to start finding ways to defend myself—and these comments were my best defensive weapons.

So, I found the student who claimed to have witnessed the incident. He had graduated three years ago and was now studying at a university in another city. I remembered him from back then: tall and skinny, wearing glasses, very attentive in my class, and his work was always outstanding. But in his eyes, I could always see a lingering sense of insecurity and fear, and that hadn't changed. I clicked on his profile picture on the forum and opened a private message with him. I asked:

"Did you really see what happened?"

"No, I was traveling at the time. I just happened to see someone talking bad about our school online, so I came to express my own opinion."

"What if someone falsely claimed that a teacher killed a student? Would you still be willing to testify?"

"Of course, I would. I have a weakness: I always stand up for justice when I see injustice. I cannot stand people spouting lies, especially when they hurt my teachers. Over the years, I've seen too many people who never reflect on themselves; they only push the blame onto others. In my opinion, even if such people died, they should still be held accountable. Otherwise, if people could just die to avoid punishment after doing something wrong, everyone would start doing it."

We continued chatting for a while. He said he liked my paintings, liked my classes, and liked me, and he was grateful for the guidance I had given him, which had given him the opportunity to succeed. Therefore, he was willing to testify for me. I replied that I was glad he had been in my school and my class and that I was happy he was willing to contribute to justice on behalf of his alma mater. Three days after our conversation, he returned to his hometown, and we went to a snack street together to have hotpot. When I took out my wallet to pay, he quickly and nervously pulled out the cash he had already prepared, his expression and movements like a child caught in the act.

Later, he said he wanted to take a walk around the campus, and I happily agreed. We walked toward the grand school gates, stepped onto the track of the sports field, and passed by one teaching building after another. As we walked, we chatted about people and events from the past in our class. The lively schoolyard during recess made him raise his voice, but as the class bell rang and the playground fell silent, his voice became as calm and slow as his footsteps. I found myself staring at the little birds on the school wall in a daze—I had spent twenty years within these walls, and yet I was less free than these birds that came and went as they pleased. Then again, perhaps this bird, like me, had been aimlessly wandering within the school grounds for twenty years. Or maybe the bird from twenty years ago had already turned to dust, and the one before me now was its offspring, trapped by the same fate.

I asked myself whether my fate and the bird's were ultimately the same or completely different. Neither the bird nor I could provide an answer until a speeding car hurtled toward the student walking beside me. Then I realized that the two options were not mutually exclusive—nothing that happened on this land was happening for the first time and would fall into cycles of repetition. Just as generations of birds had circled in the same skies, I, too, had witnessed death time and time again, only to forget it until the next one arrived. The difference between the bird and me was that my fate was far more complex. So, when this car with the scent of death approached, my instincts told me that today, he might not be my student, nor a man who secretly admired his female teacher, but he had to be my shield for self-protection today. So I stepped forward to push him away, watching the car crash into the wall and come to a stop—it was an action taken without any conscious thought. The politics teacher, also acting on instinct, walked to his car to inspect the shattered headlight. He began shouting angrily at the student, only to pause, once again instinctively, to express his guilt and apologies to me.

I asked the young man, "Are you okay?" He nodded and smiled at me, his eyes full of unguarded innocence. I smiled back, hiding the immense relief in my heart—a feeling identical to what I felt at the end of tonight's banquet. After returning home, my body gradually felt heavy, so I took a tired bath and went straight to bed. I had a dream that was both real and unreal: in the dream, I woke up on the long bench in my childhood home and heard a commotion outside the door. When I opened the door, I found myself in a private room in a hotel, surrounded by a group of my high school classmates, toasting and chatting around a round table. My first love from high school was sitting directly across from me. Upon seeing me, he stood up, bypassed all the classmates, and came to my side, shyly yet solemnly taking my hand and saying:

"You must learn to let it go."

I was a bit dazed but full of questions without knowing where to start. I asked him, "What should I let go of?"

He lowered his head and scratched the back of his head. "Never mind, maybe I cannot let go either."

I chuckled softly. For some reason, I did not

intend to press the matter further. He led me into the lavish private room, where the clinking of glassware and porcelain dishes was crisp, but the conversations were muddled. He pulled out a chair for me to sit in, and I nervously greeted the old classmates around me—I seemed to have forgotten some of their names, remembering only faint anecdotes from high school. To ease the awkwardness, I brought up these trivial stories, only to find that everyone seemed to have forgotten these insignificant memories completely.

I felt a bit lost. My first love had noticed the subtle change in my expression, so he placed a piece of sweet and sour pork ribs on my plate and moved a steaming plate of stir-fried noodles in front of me, intentionally changing the subject:

"I remember you loved eating this."

"After all these years, you still remember," I sighed.

He did not notice the tears forming in my eyes. He continued to ask me:

"How have you been lately?"

So, I began to tell him the story of my life after graduating high school—starting from the vows we made to each other after graduation, to my entering the workforce, to witnessing the deaths of several students, and finally, to receiving the honor of being named "Provincial Model Teacher for Ethics." However, I left out any mention of what happened between me and the principal. When I finished, I realized that all my high school classmates had quietly left at some point, leaving only a table full of greasy dishes behind. My first love still sat beside me, listening to my story in silence. I glanced outside the window—outside, the endless night had turned into bright midday. I was surprised at how quickly time had passed and began to wonder if I had talked too long, afraid I had exhausted his patience. So, I asked him:

"Why are you willing to listen to so many of my stories? I feel like what I've been saying is quite boring."

He quickly finished the last bit of food in his bowl, wiped his mouth, and told me:

"Actually, I do not know either. I was just thinking that back then, I was so ordinary, like a rat hiding in the sewer—no one paid attention to me, and maybe no one even wanted to. And you... you were ordinary too, right? We were both so ordinary, but our stories turned out so vastly different, and that's why I want to keep listening to you."

I lowered my head, staring at the plates in front of me, and said, "In fact, all of our stories are the same. These stories happened to me, and they'll happen to others too. Maybe even the world itself is a cycle, not to mention insignificant beings like us. An invisible hand always sweeps each of us along in a certain direction, and none of us can escape."

He replied, "Every person's story is different. Some people are participants, some are spectators, and some are narrators. Some people's paths cross with ours by chance and then separate again, while others are like parallel lines that never intersect. Some create stories, while others are created by them. Some people receive love, some give love, and some never encounter love at all. And some people, like you, still have the chance to tell their stories, while others never will, like me."

I sighed and said, "Yeah, in our lifetime, we meet many people, including ourselves. We come to know them, and eventually, we part ways, never crossing paths again." As I was lost in these thoughts, I saw him stand up from his chair, walk straight toward the door, and leave without looking back, leaving me behind, desperately calling for him to stay.

I suddenly woke up, realizing that even beautiful dreams could turn into nightmares. At that moment, I remembered he indeed no longer had the chance to tell his story—he had died in a car accident long ago. He had been trapped by a heavy rain one night, and since then, he never invited me to have sweet and sour pork ribs or stir-fried noodles again.

Perhaps, like him, I too had been trapped in some rainy night, dying in a car crash of my own.

A Red Balloon

I

Ever since middle school, I loved erasing weekend mornings, sleeping straight from late at night until noon. Mornings were a time I never wanted to face, so every weekend, the first rays of sunlight were deliberately kept out by my blackout curtains. After graduating from college and starting my job, Friday afternoons had become my favorite time—I would cook a meal, waiting for my beloved to return to our small home. After eating a meal, either casually prepared or cooked with care, we would choose a popcorn movie to watch, then make love, sleep, and the next time we opened our eyes, the sun would be shining brightly on a new day.

To me, this atmosphere was what I called "home." Here, I could immerse myself in everything around me, brainwashing myself to ignore all the pressures of study and work. I first realized this when I was in my sophomore year of college. At that time, most of my classmates' college days were filled with sleeping and playing games, so my girlfriend and I worked part-time to earn money and rented a small apartment near the school, partly to study hard for a good job, but also because we both enjoyed this little world of just the two of us.

I still remember that the place we rented was very small, which was just a one-bedroom apartment. The kitchen was so tiny that we had to duck under the range hood while cooking; our arms would be busy in the kitchen while our hips had to remain idle outside. We used the living room as our study, with two desks and two simple bookshelves filled with countless textbooks. Every time we closed the door behind us, the outside world seemed instantly cut off, and I could quietly indulge in imagining our future—we would have stable jobs, get married, have a child, own a house, retire peacefully, and watch the next generation follow the same path.

I believed I had no grand ambitions, so I never thought there was anything wrong with this kind of thinking. I had shared my vision of the future with my girlfriend; she would first laugh and say I was always so conventional, then snuggle into my arms. I missed those times; although they weren't carefree, in retrospect, they were the closest I had ever come to paradise. I believe it was paradise because we had been through hell together. She was my high school classmate, then we became desk mates, secret lovers; after we entered university, we became a couple, and later, she became my wife and the mother of our child. To her, I was a classmate, a desk mate, a boyfriend, a husband, a father, the pillar of our home, and the support she depended on in life.

Sometimes, in the middle of the night, I would

still wake up suddenly from a dream. When I was slightly awake, I would take a deep breath and tell myself that the past stories were over. If I managed to fall asleep again, I would feel fortunate the next morning; but if I could not, I would find myself playing a montage in my mind, randomly arranging all the bits and pieces of our life together.

In this montage, I would hazily return to the time when we sat together in class. I would arrive early every morning to wait for her, and then we would exchange the breakfasts we hadn't had time to eat. Sometimes, we would also swap the homework we hadn't finished the day before. I clearly remember she especially liked tofu pudding and shepherd's purse buns in the morning, while I often bought fried noodles and soy milk on my way to school. Our lovelorn homeroom teacher, on the other hand, seemed to have combined our preferences—every morning, he would carry a bag of soy milk and a bag of buns, taking a bite of the bun, drinking a sip of soy milk, while walking to the classroom.

Love was like a carefully crafted poem; when the poet began to compose, everything started to set the stage for the eventual climax. As soon as the poet places the first word on the page, the poem's melody begins. I could not remember exactly when I first started to like her—or rather, to love her—but I did remember clearly the moment when our love erupted; and at that moment, love became a synonym for filth.

Back in high school, to save money on breakfast, I would only buy a portion of plain fried noodles, while she would get dumplings stuffed with shepherd's purse, which we would swallow down with plain water. When she took a bite of my fried noodles and I took a bite of her dumpling, the homeroom teacher's gaze instantly fixed on us. He said that girls who fell in love during school would either become prostitutes, soliciting customers on the street with clothes that barely covered their breasts and lower body, or urinating on the busy streets like homeless stray dogs; while boys would become losers who took drugs or be sexually promiscuous. He did not choose to tell anyone about the breakfast exchange between her and me, but told my and her parents the scenes he imagined vividly: my girlfriend and I took off our clothes in a cramped little motel room, she spread her legs impatiently, and I could not wait to have sex with her, even without putting on a condom. Fortunately, her parents did not completely believe what the teacher said—after a brief anger, they suddenly remembered that the teacher could not have witnessed all this; unfortunately, my parents hesitated for a moment and decided to believe the teacher's vivid description.

The teacher had confidently listed the evidence

he had. My girlfriend had asked the physical
education teacher for leave on the grounds of
dysmenorrhea, and the corner of the sanitary napkin
package in her pocket was shyly exposed—this was
direct evidence that she was a slut; I had
accidentally spilled water on my crotch while
drinking water, and then passed by the teacher's
office door—this was a direct manifestation of my
high sexual desire and shamelessness. He took
photos of the evidence, sorted them out, put them in
a yellow kraft paper envelope, and then showed
them to our parents; although my parents also
doubted that I ejaculated anytime and anywhere in a
crowded classroom, they also believed that a good
girl should not announce her dysmenorrhea to the
world—So, her promiscuity had served as evidence
of my impropriety, and my shamelessness had
corroborated her depravity. These evidences
tortured me day after day. I thought of countless
reasons to refute in my mind, but unfortunately the
water stains on my pants had long evaporated, and
no one could prove whether she had
dysmenorrhea—Of course, no one was willing to
prove anything; after all, watching the fire from the
other side of the river is always more interesting
than being in the flames oneself. I knew very well
that if I were to lay bare all my thoughts, every
word I said would have been considered twisted
reasoning, and if I refused to admit to any of the

accused sins, or even if I admitted them but not with enough sincerity and straightforwardness, it would only add malicious intent to an already unforgivable crime. If I did somehow possess enough ironclad evidence to prove that these accusations were utterly groundless, another charge would be added against me: "defiance of authority." This crime was far more severe than debauchery—it encompassed the sin of licentiousness and further predicted that I would commit even graver offenses later in life.

"Does love require the blessing of others?"

I had always asked myself, but never her. My answers to myself were always contradictory: when I saw newlyweds in their wedding dresses and suits, I thought that blessings were essential—even the crude toasts and drinking games at a wedding became somehow elegant. But when I woke up from my memories, I would tell myself that when all eyes converge on a single point, those at the focal point become nothing more than others' gossip, or even objects of a curse. In my view, weddings and funerals seem no different. People start to joke and laugh through their tears, comment on the food served at the banquet, casually use the napkins on the table to wipe the oil from their lips, and finally leave, patting their bellies. Some might complain that the food was not good, while others judge the appearance of the newlyweds. In short, blessings are a luxury that I believe no one is truly fortunate enough to receive.

I had never thought that the "Wutai Poetry Case" had never ended, only that the main character had changed from Su Shi to me. Yet I envied the great poet—he was lucky to be exiled to a secluded place where he could ponder over the ancient past at Red Cliff, while I could only drown in this meaningless clamor, lamenting endlessly. I spitefully told myself just to live my own life and also decided to remain an atheist for life, as countless facts had proven that gods were powerless in the face of misfortune, and the blessings of others were equally useless. At least, I could do something myself—perhaps this also proved that gods were created by humans.

Since gods cannot cleanse sins, humans instinctively create a god that is capable of doing so, although that being may not necessarily be called "God." My sins were cleansed by an admission letter to a prestigious university—I called this piece of paper an indulgence, the price being my time, sweat, and tears, and the grades on the paper measured how much of my sins had been forgiven. My girlfriend also received a similar indulgence, though it bore a different buyer's name. I could feel the teachers' disappointment—they believed I should have spent my life in prison, or at the very least become a disgrace to my family due to my failures, but this indulgence had made them lose the bet they had placed with themselves. I still remember the "celebration banquet" at graduation, where the teachers stood to toast the students who had been accepted into second-tier universities but only clinked their glass bottoms against mine, awkwardly congratulating my "success." I knew that at that moment, in their words, I had become their genuine student, even one they could feel proud of, but in their hearts, I was nothing more than a cheater who had ruined a perfect bet. Was this formal politeness important? I used to think it was not, just like when I faced injustice and told myself: the road is walked by oneself, and the praise or criticism of others means nothing to me. But I quickly changed my mind—sorrow and anger in life are forms, joy and ease are also forms, but when they mix together, these forms define the theme and content of life.

From the moment I received my indulgence, my parents' resentment toward me vanished instantly, replaced by concern and affection. I was somewhat unaccustomed to this change, so I often went out to spend time with my girlfriend, either buying some skewers from a roadside stand or taking a nap under the shade by the lake. If I had done this in the past, I would probably have been described as a born criminal mingling with a promiscuous prostitute, but now this behavior had become the necessary socializing of two successful people. I asked my girlfriend if I had changed. Unaware of my intention, she replied without hesitation, "No." But I felt I had changed—humans are social animals; if those around someone deem them lowly, then they are lowly; if deemed noble, then they are noble. Those who are lowly naturally lead a lowly life, while those who are noble naturally receive others' respect. This is the law of the jungle, although people no longer acknowledge its applicability out loud, yet it is the reality I have witnessed with my own eyes.

Thus, I knew I should strive to adapt to my new identity—the first college student in the family, a typical case of a prodigal son returning home, the pride and hope of my parents, and proof of my school's achievements. Then this identity was further elevated to a talented individual who had achieved success and fame, a model for the children of relatives and neighbors to emulate. I gradually began to enjoy this process; I knew that now that I had become a successful person, I had to live by this identity because I did not want to reclaim the identity of a failure. Gradually, I could lean back on the sofa at home and tell my mother what I wanted to eat that day; I no longer needed to pretend to politely refuse the red envelopes from my relatives.

Graduation season is always filled with the stench of money. "Those are their indulgence, redeeming the mockery and contempt they once had for me. The amount in the red envelopes determines the speed and extent of my forgiveness," I told myself while counting the cash in the envelopes. For those relatives who stuffed a few wrinkled old bills into the envelopes, I urged my parents to cut ties with them. For those who gave me a thick stack of crisp, sequential new bills, I accepted their toasts at the banquet. While the clinking of glasses and noisy conversations were never my interest, I could still enjoy the respect I had never experienced before—the kind I had never felt since I fell in love with my girlfriend. What made me even happier was that I could witness, amidst the noisy banquet, the hollow facade of middle-aged couples who had never truly loved each other, observe them nearly come to blows over a mere two hundred yuan, and see those couples, who hadn't had sex in ten years, harboring ulterior motives, each trying to secure a bigger share of the assets in a potential divorce. And the tales they recounted about others seemed more flavorful than the delicacies on the dining table— some men hid a few dozen yuan in their shoes and socks, saving up a hundred to go out whoring; some women squandered their husband's wages, taking younger men to motels; some relatives, though impoverished, would still mock others for only drinking hundred-yuan-per-bottle liquor; and some young female relatives, claiming to be daughters of wealthy families, would willingly turn to prostitution just for the thrill of it, calling it "experiencing the cold and warmth of the human world."

Every time I heard such stories, I would suppress my smile and pretend to be playing with my phone. Now, it was my turn to mock these losers: they did not understand love, they lacked the ability to raise their children properly, and they were unable to grasp any perspectives beyond the law of the jungle. Their lives were no different from those of pigs, sheep, cats, or dogs—this description is not intended to insult or demean them but rather to explain a seemingly complex fact in the simplest language. Their love is merely about finding a mate of the opposite sex, mating, and producing offspring—nothing more. Were it not for national policies, they would likely repeat this process endlessly. Their parenting consists of nothing more than ensuring their children are fed and clothed, just as a mother dog instinctively nurses her pups. Their definition of success is merely to live with arrogance, akin to the behaviors of wild dogs vying to be the alpha in their packs. To these people, chastity is an offensive weapon; whenever someone crosses the red line in their minds, they wield it to attack others. Yet, they have no regard for their own "chastity"—most people strictly enforce a set of rules on others while adhering to a different set of flexible, ever-changing rules themselves. In my eyes, they are not even as respectable as prostitutes, for at least prostitutes do not use chastity to constrain others. I told my parents that if they continued associating with such people, I could turn against them on their behalf. My parents compromised and at least stopped interacting with them in my presence, and I enjoyed the pleasure of victory. Thus, in the three months following the college entrance exam, I took my first steps into the adult world. I was smug, subconsciously believing I had already learned how to live in this new world. This most elementary foray led me to position myself as a "successful person." I was fully aware that this success was only temporary and that there would be more challenges ahead, so the creed "I must be a successful person" was deeply engraved into my soul.

My girlfriend's life, however, seemed much more peaceful—I once described her as someone who was "neither delight in external gains, nor grieve over personal losses." My parents and relatives might have felt that I had grown up, so they no longer avoided such topics around me. Her parents, however, cherished her innocence, so her ears were never filled with these outlandish yet true stories, especially those involving relationships between men and women. After I shared with her the stories I had heard, I asked her what her ideal life was, but she could not answer. I had expected her to say, "At least not to live like those relatives," but she only slightly raised her eyes to the sky, thought for a moment, and replied:

"I just want to be an ordinary person, like everyone else."

"Yeah, it's good to be an ordinary person," I sighed, then found myself lost in contemplation and yearning for the word "success." What should be the definition of an "ordinary person"? In my mind, an ordinary person should live an ordinary life, with ups and downs, love and hate, enough to eat and drink, opportunities to speak, a job, a family, and children. But on second thought, such a life seemed like a luxury—take me, for instance: I once had neither the right to love nor even the right to speak for myself. So, what exactly is an ordinary person? Only "success" can grant these ordinary opportunities, turning someone into an ordinary person. As soon as this idea took root, I realized that two ordinary people cannot coexist; only when one ordinary person steps on another can the one standing on top truly qualify as an ordinary person.

I did not continue to ask my girlfriend what her idea of an "ordinary person" was. The question was too cruel—if I really pursued it, my actions would be akin to dragging a little girl living in a fairytale into a war-torn quagmire and ordering her to charge. She told me that her family did not have many relatives, but she had heard of similar things happening. She quickly sensed my curiosity, and she began to speak at length, almost without pause—as if she had never been so talkative before, and had never felt entitled to jest, for, in her subconscious, possessing something as delightful as love was immoral, even sinful. She gave many examples, like how a relative's child had stolen their grandparents' retirement money to buy scalped concert tickets, only to end up watching the show through binoculars from a hotel across the street; or how another relative's child mocked a classmate who had jumped to their death, only to be overheard by the deceased's parents and beaten half to death.

Comedy and tragedy can refer to the same event—when you are an outsider, it becomes comedy; when you are involved, it becomes tragedy. I seemed to be neither an outsider nor a participant, so my conflicted expression and wandering gaze were soon noticed by my girlfriend. She asked me what was wrong, and I replied:

"I am a bit envious of you."

I despised the turbulence I had experienced in life, and I could not achieve the same calmness as she had. The tone of her narration sounded like a newsreader's detached delivery or an old hermit living in seclusion, sipping cloudy wine from a wooden table while casually discussing the wars of the mortal world with a friend. I imagined she might have already integrated this style into her own world—a world where everything was as calm as still water, where no one played with words, and people quietly observed the faint ripples around them; where everyone and everything was but a passerby in the course of life. Perhaps my girlfriend once had the ability to share these anecdotes with me accompanied by her enchanting laughter, but now, she seemed like a spring that had been compressed under a boulder for eighteen years, and once the boulder had crumbled, the spring could no longer stretch back out.

She said that tragedy could also be used for amusement, even if it happened to oneself. Tragedy, in itself, is worthless; no one remembers the strange answers we wrote in our elementary school unit tests ten years ago, and if they do, it's only because it was amusing enough to be memorable. But back then, when we saw a red cross on the test papers, did not we see it as a stain on our lives? That red cross was not just a stain; it could have seemed like a catastrophe comparable to the end of the world.

I said, "For some kids, it really is the end of the world."

She replied, "But for other kids, it might just be a minor episode in life."

Yet, in reality, when a tragedy can be used for amusement, it will be repeatedly brought out from its buried coffin, displayed and toyed with, used as a seasoning for family gatherings, as proof to punish someone, or as a testament to someone's deep experience. Those tragedies that remain buried, never unearthed, slowly take root and sprout. Eventually, people only notice them when they have grown into towering trees, but no one thinks of them as the tiny seeds they once were—of course, no one cares what they used to be like.

II

My favorite ancient saying is "one general's success is built upon thousands of bodies." It's not the cruelty of the phrase that I like, but rather its bluntness and honesty. I also appreciate how it has helped me understand the true nature of success.

So, during a chance visit to my ancestors' graves, I once went to a cemetery with my wife. It was my first and, so far, only time visiting such a place. I found it hard to connect emotionally with those ancestors I had never met, but I was curious about what a scene of "thousands of bones" truly looked like. In the cemetery, I happened to see an old couple; they were my neighbors from ten years ago, who were visiting their son's grave on the second day after being released from prison. I dared not approach them, as there seemed to be an invisible magnetic field around the couple; whenever I got closer, this field would pull at my heart. I did not greet them; I just squinted from afar at their son's tombstone, where the two sets of numbers—his birth date and the date of his death— stood out, glinting in the morning dew, while their silver hair seemed to blend with the color of the tombstone.

"He was seventeen, and he will never grow older."

As this thought floated through my mind, I

asked myself, what should the tone of this sentence be? Perhaps it should be sorrowful, perhaps it should suggest relief, or maybe it should be mocking. Anyway, asking this question revealed my own cold heart. I quietly walked past the elderly couple from behind and continued on my way. As I walked, I recalled my thoughts about this land before entering the cemetery: some stones, either delicate or plain, neatly arranged on the ground; beneath them, fragmented ashes, with maggots were crawling in the remains. At night, there would always be wandering, unvisited spirits, conversing among themselves but unable to change the course of life in the world. Of course, I had also imagined more beautiful scenes—such as standing in the cemetery, seeing distant mountains, hearing birds singing in the trees, touching wildflowers growing from cracks in the stones, or even sensing the ocean waves crashing against the shore miles away.

However, when I actually arrived, all the imagined scenes vanished, replaced by the reality before me. I walked on the hard concrete ground, passing by one neat tombstone after another, my eyes scanning the death dates engraved on them, silently calculating how long the souls beneath the tombs had been separated from their bodies. Here, there was no difference between those who died of old age and those who died young; everyone was just a handful of dirt under the ground. It was then that I realized that the most regrettable aspect of death is that both the soul and the body are irreplaceable, and death means that a particular combination of soul and body will never appear again.

"It's good to leave. The world is not beautiful, and sometimes it's even ugly. No need to come back." I silently comforted the people beneath the tombstones.

The term "a withered skeleton in a tomb" is actually a term with a hint of blessing—many people do not even have the luxury of possessing a lonely grave and a few skeletons. And when the last person who remembers them is gone, they truly vanish with the wind, leaving not a trace behind. Anyway, it seems that no one insists on searching for those traces, either. In the cemetery, I saw a man playing the violin in front of a tombstone; it was not bad, but it was not particularly moving either. In front of another tombstone was a large box of jelly filled with orange segments, scattered with small, nameless snacks nearby. A slightly wilted bouquet of roses lay on the path, seemingly snatched away by a gust of wind from the grave and discarded. What else can the living do for the deceased besides buying these things? I could not come up with an answer.

When we left the cemetery, the elderly couple was also leaving. They walked slowly ahead, and I held my wife's hand as we followed from a distance. Was their son's death meaningful? Perhaps, perhaps not. Was his death right or wrong? Maybe right, maybe wrong. As an outsider, it's hard to judge his actions, especially after witnessing countless separations between life and death. However, I know that meaningless and wrongful deaths make up the majority: some people die in accidents, which are pointless and avoidable; others are murdered, and even if the killer is sentenced to death, what do their lives exchange for? Nothing.

I once had a dream about death. It was a strange dream—countless young women with beautiful figures gathered in a circular theater, laughing and chatting as they circled around. The large speakers in the theater played eerie music, seemingly describing raging flames burning wildly. A performance was taking place on the stage that I could not understand; all I could see were faceless people picking up guns and shooting those around them, mechanically repeating the act of pulling the trigger until everyone lay on the ground. The women in the stands cheered for the bloodshed and death, celebrating each echo of a bullet leaving the chamber with the explosive music, loudly mocking the supposedly fake blood and flesh on stage, while throwing countless flowers and gold and silver toward me, who stood dumbfounded.

I woke up, finding that the sky was already

beginning to lighten, and my wife was still sleeping soundly next to me. I could not fathom the logic of this dream, but I felt a strong urge to record the dream and write it down. As I prepared to put pen to paper, fear crept into my heart. At that moment, my fear was a mixture: the noise, the flickering lights, the scattered flesh, the exclamations and laughter of the crowd, the gazes of the onlookers... Dreams are inherently intangible, but it seemed to correspond to every moment I had experienced, forcibly transforming those experiences into elements that composed my fear.

The intensity of one's fear is not determined by its initial cause, much like the chicks in a chicken farm—a brief clap of thunder might only cause a few of them to shiver, but that tiny tremor would spread to every corner of the flock, eventually leaving no companion unaffected. Whether they were scared to death or trampled to death by their companions, the cause was just an inconspicuous thunderclap; the real culprit was the surrounding peers. I have always felt that I am no different from the chicks—I accept fear, and I transmit fear. As a police officer, a corpse is certainly frightening, but I had mentally prepared myself; facing fear is part of my duty. I've seen gory scenes and even looked forward to having the chance to handle bloody cases, so I always willingly rushed to the front. I believe I am not a psychopath, but rather, I am constantly chasing after the "success" that I dream of—this has never changed.

Yet, once I hover at the edge of fear, it can suddenly arrive without warning. When I parted the crowd of onlookers and reached the corpse, my heart was calm. I could calmly face the eyes of the dead and calmly set up a cordon around the scene, but I did not want to hear the deceased's story or others' evaluations of them—the dead are not frightening, nor are the living; what is terrifying is the state of hovering between life and death. I find it hard to describe this feeling—when a corpse is laid before you, it becomes an object, lifeless and speechless, so I can face it indifferently; but then the onlookers would evaluate such an object, making it feel as though it had been given a story and had come back to life, turning it into a living person again.

"Must be poor grades that led to the jump; dying like this is a waste."

"Probably went crazy from playing video games; why else would anyone jump?"

"What's so unusual about a student dying? One less competitor for the college entrance exam."

"Kids this age just die over some love affair. If they're dating at this age, who knows what trouble they'll cause in the future."

This is the script that the onlookers write for a corpse—they're eager to voice their creation, unwilling even to take the time to confirm if this is indeed a corpse or merely a dying person. I shifted my gaze from the child lying on the ground and swept it across the surrounding crowd. Some wore plastic slippers, pacing around, their footsteps scraping against the concrete, producing grating noises; some seemed to have rushed out without even washing up to see the spectacle; a few children had also come over, covering their eyes with their hands, but leaving small gaps between their fingers, wanting to look but too afraid to see. But most people were busy speculating about what had happened, while chatting with strangers around them. Their low murmurs were deafening to me; I tried to block out all the noise, but to no avail.

Their words made me imagine myself as the deceased. If I were the one lying here now, what would they say about me? I guessed, in their mouths, I would be the lecherous bad kid from before, or perhaps just an insignificant ant. But I was sure there would not be a shred of compassion in their words. At that moment, before my eyes was bright sunshine; cheerful birds pecked at rice grains spilling out of bags on the ground; the clattering sound of pots and pans came from a restaurant nearby, and a water truck played cheerful music as it washed the dust from the road. Everything in the real world remained as usual. But if the soul of the deceased could detach from this shell, what would it see? Perhaps a dark night pressing down on its former vessel, or the people around it shooting a thousand arrows, pinning it firmly to the ground, allowing no escape or hiding.

"Respect for the dead" has never been a tradition, let alone a standard for people's behavior. Often, this phrase is only uttered when someone curses or mocks a deceased person, and its very mention implies that the person in question was not respected in life and can only find peace in death—simply because they are gone, and people do not like to be bothered to waste more breath condemning them. Besides, the most likely reason for a lack of respect for the living is a low status during their lifetime. Whenever people mention emperors or generals, regardless of their deeds, whether they leave a legacy or a trail of blood, they often say, "Let history judge their merits and faults." But when a small, insignificant person is wiped off the face of the earth, their experiences are no longer worth discussing; even talking about them is considered a waste of time.

Realizing this, my fear intensified. My colleagues were nearby, questioning witnesses, and while I was lost in thought, an ambulance took the child to the hospital. I stared at the bloodstains left on the ground, feeling an unsettling sense that a soul really existed, now merged into that pool of blood. The crowd around me grew larger, repeatedly

reciting their improvised scripts. As different
versions of the story collided, people instinctively
began comparing the merits of each. Truth did not
captivate anyone; on the contrary, the weight of
truth seemed feather-light, scarcely noticeable even
when it fell right before their eyes. I stood in the
middle of the crowd, helplessly enduring these
comments, even though they were not directed at
me. I did not know what to do; all I could do was
suppress the urge to step forward and force
everyone to shut up.

Instinctively, I took a step back and gripped
the yellow caution tape. It was no longer just a cold,
plastic barrier but a boundary separating life from
death. I felt as if I were standing on the edge of a
cliff, with a vibrant city behind me and a burning
abyss in front of me. I feared falling off that cliff,
but I feared even more the ridicule from those
standing on the edge. Yet, I kept reminding myself
that I would face death eventually, and perhaps, by
then, I would no longer be afraid; what the living
say might not matter so much, especially since they,
too, will face this day.

My thoughts and the murmurs of the crowd
were abruptly silenced by a loud shout:

"Counter-revolutionary[24] scum, good
riddance!"

The shout came from a brawny man, pointing
at the bloodstains and shattered glass on the ground,

his eyes bulging with anger, his saliva spraying over every inch of ground in front of him. His voice exploded like a bomb amidst the crowd, its power instantly plunging the surroundings into silence—an even deeper silence than I had ever experienced. I stared intently at the shouting man, and my mind quickly simulated the scene that might follow: he might suddenly lose his temper, rush at me, attack me or someone else, and then my colleagues might come over to restrain him and handcuff him. When my thoughts returned to normal, I took the time to observe the man in front of me: he was burly, wearing glasses, with the smell of alcohol on his breath and a flushed face, indicating that he had just been drinking. Instinctively, I placed my right hand on my baton, waiting for him to break through the caution tape and attack.

However, the imagined confrontation did not happen, and the task of calming the man down was taken up by two middle-aged women outside the caution tape. One woman gently patted the man's shoulder, while the other nodded and bowed, soothingly stroking his hand, trying her best to calm him down. Passing children greeted him, humbly calling him "teacher." Awkwardly, I removed my hand from the baton—it was no longer a weapon, but a symbol of my buried naivety. I chastised myself for forgetting:

"Did you forget how the lowly used to flatter

the high and mighty?"

The man was coaxed and cajoled by my colleagues until he calmed down. Then, he got into our police car, or rather, he was politely ushered into it. I looked on, puzzled by the scene unfolding before me, unable to understand why it was happening. A colleague noticed my confusion and pointed at another man behind him—he was the current principal of my old high school. I did not approach him—not because I had to maintain order at the scene, but because I did not want a sudden conversation to trigger memories of the past. I quickly understood my colleague's hint, but the deference shown to the principal and the teachers felt out of place in such a tragic crime scene. It was like seeing a group of bare-chested men happily eating ice-cold watermelon in a snow-blocked winter, or a group shivering in thick coats under the scorching sun of August.

I had a reasonably good impression of this principal, but upon closer reflection, I realized that my favorable opinion of him was not due to any particular shining deeds of his. Instead, it stemmed from a common yet often overlooked principle: people have high standards for the weak and low standards for the strong. In other words, weighing the pros and cons is part of human nature, so people often dare not speak against the crimes of the powerful but will readily criticize the flaws of the weak. It took me a while to find evidence in my memory to support my good impression of him. I had once personally arrested my high school teacher—the one who had fabricated stories about me. He was caught in a room with purple bedside lamps, sharing a bed with two young women. My body camera clearly captured the changes in his expression: from panic and anxiety to tearful and pitiful, and upon recognizing me, he became loquacious. But after I rejected his attempt to bribe me, his expression turned to resentment and dissatisfaction. He started with a pleading tone, asking me to remember his past kindness as a teacher, then shifted to a commanding tone, urging me to accept his money.

At this moment, the taste of victory was far more enticing than a few bills. If there were no body cameras, I imagine I would have first taken the money from his hand, then humiliated him, and finally arrested him according to the law and regulations. Did the principal do anything? It seems he did nothing at all. And my favorable impression of him was precisely because he did nothing—when the teacher under his command was arrested, he never pleaded for him, and we proceeded with the matter in an orderly fashion. I longed day and night for him to be disgraced and lose his job, and indeed, that was what happened. While I was wildly rejoicing, I realized that my atheist beliefs had experienced a brief moment of wavering. I asked myself, "Is this karma?" I answered myself: yes, and no. Yes, because he happened to fall into my hands, which would make his psychological wounds harder to heal, perhaps leaving him trapped in regret for the rest of his life. No, because only after experiencing power and respect myself did I understand him—seeing teenage romance as a heinous crime was his instinct, and this instinct was precisely what he believed his supreme authority granted him. In his subconscious, any sexual behavior is a kind of resource; whether it is a secret crush that people dare not speak out or explicit sex, these behaviors should be monopolized by him, but if these behaviors are not under his control at some point, it constitutes a provocation and threat to his authority. As for his own act of soliciting prostitutes, he considered it a reasonable way to spend his power once he had monopolized it—at least, that's what he believed. After all, no one, once they've gained power, refrains from abusing it; everyone is the same in this regard.

When I learned the outcome of the teacher's case, I made a point of buying a bottle of good wine with my wife, along with some braised beef and pig's trotters that she usually would not splurge on. In a slightly tipsy state, we chatted and laughed, then had a vigorous round of lovemaking. However, when the uncontrollable joy finally ebbed away, I felt a twinge of loss—I worried that after experiencing such genuine happiness, would I still be able to endure a life devoid of ripples? I could imagine the life of someone who once wielded power over life and death sinking into melancholy and emptiness after losing that authority; it would mean that person could no longer provide me with new pleasures.

Perhaps my worry was unwarranted—the calm life was soon met with disturbance. I had witnessed the child's death, seen the evidence and the faces of the people involved, and had overheard bits and pieces of clues: the shattered glass outside the window, reports of teachers committing robbery, the heavy label of "anti-Party elements," and the looks from the students around the neighborhood... I believed that my colleagues could see what had happened immediately; after all, even a community cop like me could notice some signs, let alone the veteran detectives with much more experience. The difference between them and me was in the amount of experience, but I believed that our intelligence was not essentially different. When I found out that the school personnel had left with the police folks in high spirits, while the deceased's parents were detained, I understood the whole truth—this was the natural law of "survival of the fittest". The higher predators in the food chain decide the life and death of their prey; those who cannot adapt to this reality

are ruthlessly eliminated, and "elimination" often
means literal extinction.

This law is easy to understand, but it's so
brutal that it dares not be understood. After I left the
crime scene and returned home, I saw my child
playing tirelessly on the slide in the neighborhood.
He climbed up the steps excitedly, slid down,
climbed back up, and slid down again... He found
this big toy fascinating, unaware that, in the eyes of
an adult like me, it was nothing more than a slanted
plastic board. If he knew this truth, would he still be
interested in the slide? What's more brutal is that
one day he will understand the principle behind the
slide, just as I eventually understood the laws by
which the world operates—no matter how
cautiously we treaded, we inevitably stumbled upon
harsh realities like truth. I was glad my child was
still privileged to ignore the cruelty of this world,
and he could still enjoy sliding down; but I was also
sad, knowing that this time may not be far from
disappearing forever, and I had no idea how to keep
this innocent state by my side.

The next day at work, my colleague told me
that the child had been lying on the operating table
for hours. No one knew his condition on that
table—whether he was alive or dead, in pain or
numb, filled with hatred or relieved—we, the
regular police officers, did not know; his parents did
not know; the school personnel did not know, and

even the doctors did not dare to decide whether he should be dead or alive. They could only wait for the directives from above. Waiting is always torturous; it's like a steel collar tightly fastened around the neck. Even if you know the truth lies ahead, the collar of waiting stops you from tasting its flavor.

I believe the child's pain and mine might have the same essence.

III

There was a moment when I wished that kid could hate the world and hate everything he had experienced, because everything he and I went through seemed to show that love was an unforgivable sin, while hate was a necessary condition for achieving success, so much so that hate had become a sacred emotion—not only inviolable but also something people should occasionally flaunt to show their admirable ambition. As a result, baseless hatred is everywhere, while profound love is nowhere to be found.

Unfortunately, he no longer remembered the love and hate of the past, but I had a vivid impression of the neighborhood where the tragedy occurred. The first time I came to this place, construction machinery was digging large pits in the ground. The rain from the previous night had yet to leave the holes in the earth, and the workers arrived the next day to continue their work. I watched as steel bars were tightly bound together, red bricks slowly stacked to form walls, and cement trucks arrived, unloaded, left, and returned, over and over again.

A hundred meters away from the neighborhood stood the school. When the new teaching building was completed, the role of this neighborhood was set in stone—countless parents competed to buy properties here to save their children a bit of time on their daily commute. As a community police officer responsible for this area, I knew every household: some parents bought houses here specifically for their children's education, while some wealthy people bought several apartments to rent out; some parents were away from home all year, leaving the house for their children to live in alone, while others moved in with their whole family, even if it made their daily commute to work very inconvenient.

The land on which the school sits might have been an ancient riverbed a million years ago, the dwelling place of primitive humans a hundred thousand years ago, a forest thousands of years ago, or a battlefield centuries ago. What I was certain of was that it was a cemetery forty years ago, a factory thirty years ago, a wasteland twenty years ago, and a school ten years ago. The new school gate towers twenty meters high, with an eighty-thousand-dollar boulder placed before it. The pillars displayed the school's many honors and countless photos of various officials visiting the school. Yet, to me, these visible decorations were meaningless, and the grand and imposing gate had become clichéd since the son of an old neighbor passed away—it reeked of flattery, raising its head proudly before the humble while bowing obsequiously to so-called dignitaries. Hence, I preferred to call this kind of cliché "kitsch." Kitsch has no real meaning or practical significance, but it does have purposes: it serves to flaunt hidden disgraceful deeds to the world in a different form while subtly conveying unspeakable desires to those who can understand them. Thus, all tragedies serve the desires behind kitsch.

The evidence of this kitsch was not hard to find; at least, I could spot two pieces right at the school gate: a bright red banner announced the provincial model high school title earned five years ago, while another red paper next to it advertised the centennial celebration of the school[25]. No one cares about the bloodshed behind these honors because blood is so easily wiped away—a single photo of the principal with the provincial party secretary is enough to prove that no crime ever occurred. There were even more witnesses to this kitsch—those parents flaunting their literary skills outside the cordon were living examples. But because kitsch itself serves to cover up the ugly, interpretations of the truth behind it can differ greatly, even be diametrically opposed. Just like different people reading the same novel, the light and cheerful words might hide heavy yokes, and heavy words might hide bright and hopeful freedom. So, when kitsch saturates the entire environment, it is no longer a folk art form but becomes a poison; when consumed excessively, it has irreversible side effects—creating inescapable illusions that penetrate deep into the bones.

I had witnessed these side effects, especially during investigations. The residents of the neighborhood spoke highly of the teachers involved in the case—some said their children's grades improved after entering the school, while others claimed the teachers had cured their children of early romantic relationships and internet addiction[26]. Among them, the worst evaluation of the teachers was just, "I did not see anyone jump," after which they said no more.

"Anyway, this would never happen to my child."

When a father told me this, I glimpsed the student standing behind him. The father stood at the door, slightly hunched over, occasionally nodding quickly. His daughter peeked out from a room behind him, then turned back inside without closing the door. The child's eyes were blank, and even her movements seemed robotic and unnatural. I remembered this child—she had once come crying to report that a teacher had taken her iPhone during a home visit, and now, the phone, a birthday gift, was somewhere far away. She specifically asked me not to tell her parents she had reported it because her parents believed the teacher's intention was for her good and that she should not let down the teacher's earnest efforts. I remember hypocritically promising to investigate, but after just three seconds of hesitation, I discarded the matter—when I face something I am powerless to handle, I would rather not spend any effort on it than waste time without results.

The fact that convinced me I was immune to kitsch was that I did not mock the girl's naivety and overestimation of herself; on the contrary, I felt a pang of sympathy in my heart. Immunity to kitsch also has its side effects, which I call "self-doubt." From the moment I saw the glittering shards of glass scattered all over the ground, I believed the child did not die by suicide; the chaos in the room only confirmed my suspicion. But so what? I never heard the child's parents describe the whole tragedy, or rather, all I heard was a description full of holes. All I could do was piece together the known information into what I believed was a reasonable narrative. I was just a low-level police officer, not a trained detective, so solving the case was not my job. Still, hearing so many irrelevant accounts, I could not help but doubt myself— perhaps there was something I had missed, leading me to misunderstand the suspects in my mind; perhaps they really were innocent.

Regardless of whether my assumptions about the case were right or wrong, I sneered at the parents' sense of luck—if something happens only once, it means it either never happened or has happened more than once and will continue to happen. I was sure they were under the influence of kitsch, and the poison it released was creating illusions in their minds. I secretly scoffed at them: What makes you think that what happened to others will not happen to you again? Of course, I held back from asking that question, but I imagined they might answer that they had given generous gifts or that they always chatted cheerfully with the teachers, or perhaps they trusted the teachers' character. Thinking of this, I sneered at their naivety again—as if a thick red envelope could buy a chance to survive, as if a toast at a party could earn respect, as if their gaze could penetrate human nature and discern the purity or filth deeply buried in the soul.

Looking back, although I believed I had never been tainted by kitsch, I, too, had fallen into the illusions created by it. An illusion is also a kind of disease—I do not know what to call it, but I know its aftereffects: a fear of any risk, regardless of how likely it is to come true. As long as there is the slightest risk, I will magnify it tenfold, a hundredfold. My illusion once told me that it could wield an invisible force, compelling me to do anything, and if I disobeyed, disaster would befall me and my family. I often heard that such calamity could strike at any time, and my wife often reminded me of its existence, so much so that, even though I had never seen it with my own eyes, I developed a deep-seated fear of it. In my imagination, this invisible force demanded that I blend in perfectly with everyone else, that I carry out every task assigned by my superiors without fail, and that I remain silent when I should not speak. I mocked myself; I had spent so long learning how to stand out—from learning to speak starting with "Dad" and "Mom," to writing word by word, to gradually adapting to the role of a "successful person" in the family—yet now I had to learn how to blend in naturally and unpretentiously.

The illusion also told me that humans are creatures who forget their origins. Some people curse and disdain the filthiness of sex, yet remain oblivious that they themselves are a product of sex. Some people despise lies, yet constantly allow lies to slip from their own mouths. Others once set up an unbreakable moral standard for themselves, only to discover in the end that the lofty standard was merely a shackle designed for others. This kind of forgetting may be subjective; people adjust their memories to protect themselves and adapt to their surroundings. But sometimes, this forgetting is not subjective—when people remember their "origin" but are forced to pretend to forget, or even have to destroy it with their own hands, they will experience agony. This pain feels like being torn apart from the middle of the body; when irresistible pain and an inescapable reality both exert their force on a person, the soul is torn apart. At that moment, the soul becomes a monster born from the union of an angel and a demon. The holy half of the soul will say, "Come, be loyal to the light I spread, be true to your pure heart, and be a real person." The evil half will say, "If you are seduced by the other half, you and your family will fall into eternal damnation, and everyone affected by you will curse you."

When everyone is torn apart, an unwritten rule becomes known to all: loyalty can be hypocritical and fickle, but fear is real and eternal. Thus, people become obsessed with creating fear to fabricate an extravagant reality in this otherwise vague world. I believed the world had tailored a set of fears for me—I feared losing my job; I feared my wife and child becoming homeless because of me; I feared my child would no longer be allowed to attend school; I feared my wife's parents would lose their pension due to one of my reckless decisions; I feared losing my successful image in the eyes of others; I even feared that my child's children would not be allowed to find a job in the future[27]. Whenever I felt fear, I asked myself, "What is the source of this fear?" The answer may still be my obsession with success. I long for success—at least the kind of success that people around me recognize—and so I truly succeeded. After my success, admiration from others and praise followed, but slowly these praises and admiration morphed into a kind of curse, which would never return to its original form.

This curse constantly whispered in my ear. It said, "Failure is a possibility that will always exist, and once you realize this, fear will be ever-present, even if you ultimately achieve the success you desire." Its words felt like a giant stone crushing my fragile heart, leaving me breathless. Thus, I began to envy others who could complete their tasks without any psychological burden—they were still whole, while I had to abandon part of my soul. From the outside, I was no different from those around me; we all did the same work, endured the same nature and degree of fear. The only difference was the amount of pain from the tearing within our hearts. This difference was invisible to others, and I, who bore the pain, could not prove its existence. My actions tried hard to prove that it did not exist, so when this pain was present, the grievance that accompanied the pain also existed. This grievance felt like a leech sucking my soul, sticking just above the skin. I could only allow it to feed on me— believing that when my soul was drained, I would have completed a slow and imperceptible transformation.

When this transformation was complete, I naturally put aside the case of the missing child and issued a notice of non-filing; I threw the rape and domestic violence cases back to the parties involved, letting them resolve their own matters themselves; as for cases of theft and robbery, even when I had to handle them, I could convince myself to lower their priority. At this point, I acknowledged within that the death of the old neighbor's son was my top priority; everything else could be temporarily forgotten. I had to use his life as a stepping stone for my progress; otherwise, I would become a burial companion for a corpse—such a sacrifice would be meaningless. So, I could only convince myself that his role was no longer that of a student, a child, or the son of my old neighbor, but an enemy blocking my path to success. Even if I wanted to sympathize with him, my inner fear did not allow me to take any action for my sympathy.

I overheard a young colleague saying that the case was clearly a murder, but the criminal investigation team was too lazy to do their job, only taking a few photos at the scene before heading off to drink with the school officials. An older cop nearing retirement responded, "Kid, watch your mouth. The conclusion has already been made. After working for another ten or twenty years, you'll understand that just getting by is good enough." Then another young officer said, "It's good that he died. His whole family should die. Not only do they trouble us, but they also smear his teachers and alma mater. That kid died too late." After those words, perhaps some silently agreed, while others might have silently disagreed, but no one voiced even the slightest opposition. Everyone tacitly nodded, turned around, and returned to their desks, leaving only the sound of leather shoes tapping on the tile floor, echoing for a long time.

"Let's just pretend it's all a rumor."

I convinced myself, and my wife told me the same. So, I gently closed the case file, just as I had gently closed my books after the college entrance examination. To me, the case file was no different from a high school textbook—when opened, they were the meaning of my life; but when closed, they symbolized the end of an era. Thus, an era belonging to this child had ended: he would no longer appear in this world; he would exist like all the grass, trees, insects, and fish—existing, having existed, and soon completely vanishing from the world without a trace.

At home that night, I held my son in my arms as he slept. He drooled, sleeping soundly. I thought of myself when I was his age, and I could not help but smile. I, too, had started as a child, moving forward moment by moment, becoming who I am today. Along the way, my role has sometimes been that of a superior idol, and at other times a lesser being, like a pig or a dog—or like my role in this case—both an idol and a lesser being. But it seems I have never been just a person. When I am an idol, I have the right to trample pigs and dogs underfoot and revel wildly. When I become the pig or dog, there is always an idol riding on my head, pointing and directing. I told myself that everyone was both a pig or dog and an idol. Who is my idol? The station chief, the department chief, or the municipal party secretary? And whose idol am I? The idol of those relatives at home? All these are nothing more than ethereal titles. Everyone will come to that moment of death; when that moment arrives, titles, honors, and even names will become meaningless symbols. These symbols merely represent a predetermined historical process, but they cannot change the direction of history, because when the body bearing this symbol has perished, it no longer carries responsibility. It only leaves behind the unfinished exam paper of its life for future generations, whose scores it cannot influence. I cannot complete this exam paper in my life, nor can my child—that is the truly sad part. We spend our whole lives trying to be idols, never thinking about how many people we have trampled beneath us, nor imagining how many have used us as stepping stones, nor considering that at the moment of our death, the title of idol will shatter, and the remaining fragments of memory left behind will gradually dissolve into this world.

Fortunately, the fragments left behind by the child have not yet dissolved, and my title has not yet shattered. At this point in time, I was fortunate enough to attend a banquet. Rather than calling it a banquet, it was more like an internal seminar about the answers to an exam. I had once left some marks on this exam paper, and today I was merely attending an informal social event with the "examiners." I was delighted to attend—this meant my work was recognized, which, in turn, meant that my wife did not have to worry about my career, my child was no longer in danger of losing the right to education, and the elderly in my family could continue to receive their pensions.

After enduring two hours of the noise from card games and mahjong, the banquet finally began with its opening act. The delicate blue and white porcelain wine cup felt very small in my hand, and the clear wine seemed little. But the moment the liquid entered my mouth, the intense spiciness, bitterness, sweetness, and fragrance were instantly released, penetrating every cell in my body. I instantly understood something: the cup of wine in my hand contained the entirety of the child's life— he was small, easily swallowed by us in one gulp, disappearing into nothingness; he was intense, intense enough to roar past us and let the wind behind him awaken slumbering, numb souls; he was rich, rich enough to dissolve all absurdity, baseness, and danger.

The police chief said it was all an accident. At this age, kids commit suicide either because of a love affair or due to academic pressure. The principal said that he and all of us were innocent parties caught in the middle, and no one wanted trouble. The principal's mistress said our fate had determined that we would become heroes. The principal's brother said we had won. I understood their meaning: life is a game, and winning or losing is determined by fate, which in turn is controlled by an indescribable force. This force transcends me, them, and everyone else; it is responsible for building the stage, and we are the actors imprisoned on that stage, forced to comply with the script's dictates—all love, hatred, joy, sorrow, life, and death are prearranged. Yet the actors attribute the plot's twists and turns to unforeseen random events. Meanwhile, the audience sits and watches, unaware that they, too, are part of the performance. So, who is the director of this grand show? I do not know, or rather, even if I did know, I would not dare to say, fearing that this line was not in the script and that my improvisation might ruin the entire play.

At the end of the performance, the director said to me, "You are good at writing articles, so I am letting you write the police announcement!"

He patted me on the shoulder, as if passing all his strength to me. I hesitated for a long time, but in the face of fear, I decided to be a bit clever. I did not want to lose my job, nor did I want to ruin the future of my son and even my grandchildren, but I was willing to use my writing to give his parents a sliver of hope for survival—I decided not to mention the Bible found in their home or the label of "anti-Party elements" placed on them[28]. The director stroked his chin, thought about it, and agreed with my idea, but his reasoning was that digging deeper would be too troublesome, and he was not willing to expend that much effort.

So, an official document burst forth from my pen like a clap of thunder:

Police Announcement

Recently, the City Police Department and the community police station received a report that a student fell to their death from an eighth-floor residence. This case has attracted the attention of surrounding residents. After a lawful investigation, the following information is provided to the public:

1. **Investigation Regarding the Claim by the Deceased's Parents that the Principal and Teachers Pushed the Deceased to Cause His Death**

   The investigation found that both parents of the deceased suffer from severe mental illness, and their testimonies were inconsistent and contradictory; therefore, their statements are deemed unreliable. It was confirmed that the deceased's principal and teachers had no motive to kill the deceased, and there were no eyewitnesses or any evidence supporting the parents' claims. Results from interviews indicate that the deceased's school principal and teachers have excellent reputations and no criminal records. A crime scene investigation and physical evidence examination have ruled out any criminal case. After further questioning, the parents admitted that the deceased had repeatedly attacked teachers at the school with weapons and that they fabricated the claim of "intentional murder by teachers" to demand more compensation. The deceased's parents are currently under criminal detention by the police on suspicion of fabricating rumors and causing trouble.

2. **Investigation Regarding Claims of the Deceased's Addiction to Online Games**

The investigation of the deceased's electronic devices, including phones and computers, and interviews with the deceased's classmates and relatives have confirmed that the deceased had excellent academic performance and showed no signs of game addiction. The claim of suicide due to "poor academic performance" is also unsubstantiated.

3. **Investigation Regarding Claims of Suicide Due to Romantic Relationships**

The investigation confirmed that the

deceased did have a tendency toward early romantic relationships. The police have found a suicide note, which confirmed signs of suicidal ideation before the incident. The content of the suicide note is as follows:

"I cannot be openly together with the person I love; I might as well die."

It has been proven that the deceased went through multiple breakups and reconciliations with the involved individual. The deceased had attempted suicide several times before the incident but was unsuccessful. The deceased's girlfriend confirmed that the suicide might have been due to emotional disputes.

4. **Investigation Regarding Claims of "Habitual Robbery by Teachers"**

This claim has been proven false. The local police station and the City Police Department's criminal investigation team have lawfully arrested the person who posted these claims online (female, 16 years old, a student). Her online statements, such as "The teacher stole my phone during a home visit" and "There are more victims; they habitually rob," have been confirmed as fabrications. Her motive was to vent frustration over her incorrectly graded exam, which caused the student's score to be lower than it should have been. Additionally, 19 individuals who liked her online post (all of whom are her classmates) have been detained and questioned by the police and have admitted that the claims are untrue.

The loss of a life is heartbreaking. We hereby urge all citizens not to fabricate, spread, or believe in rumors and to enhance social awareness and etiquette. The police department will resolutely investigate and handle any criminal behavior without leniency.

As I struck the final key in the quiet of the night, my body slumped heavily against the back of the chair. The seat emitted a series of irregular creaks, sounding almost like my fears momentarily squeezing out through the fissures in my soul. Above me, a gray-black moth had appeared out of nowhere, furiously hurling itself against the glass of the lightbulb, as if it could somehow claim the brightness on the other side as its own. Yet, it could neither break through the glass nor find another way in. So, after a moment of lingering, brimming with reluctant longing, it fluttered around the light for a while longer, finally seeking out a shadowed corner to settle down and sleep.

—— **THE END** ——

Afterword

This story ends here. I debated for a long time about whether to write this afterword. It did not take me much time to complete this piece, but after writing the last sentence, I felt that there was more left unsaid, yet I did not know how to begin. Eventually, I decided to write an afterword to further discuss what I've written. How should I approach this afterword? I decided to use some of the questions raised by readers after reading this novel as a starting point. I hope that through my answers, readers can gain a clearer understanding of what I intended to convey.

Q1: Why did you write the first part, "The Ripple"?

A1: From an emotional perspective, although the overall tone of the novel is dark, there is beauty even in tragedy. The protagonist's mental imagery blends reality with fantasy, yet remains overall inclined toward the beautiful, regardless of its truth. Both beautiful facts and beautiful imaginations are weapons against darkness. From an objective and rational perspective, the purpose of "The Ripple" is primarily to narrate the events from the perspective of the victimized student and to depict what kind of person the student was, ultimately prompting the reader to consider: Who destroyed all this beauty?

Q2: Why does the third part, "Breaking

Free," seem unrelated to the student's death?

A2: There are never truly and completely isolated events; everything is connected. This is one of the main themes of "Breaking Free." I have never believed that "man is inherently good," so a person can be born evil, but that might be a biological question. Exploring how a person turns into an evildoer is much more meaningful. We often notice significant events that change the course of a life, but we may overlook the small things we see, hear, and think. In reality, these major events might just be the trigger, while the details could be the true reasons for a personality change. Thus, most of this novel talks about things seemingly unrelated to the core event, but when combined, they form this story. The value system expressed by the teacher in this chapter is quite distorted, but I hope that through such depictions, readers can understand the existence of such twisted values.

Q3: Why does it seem that all the evildoers in the novel have their reasons, and some even seem innocent?

A3: People instinctively make excuses to absolve themselves of guilt, and these excuses are often referred to as "justifications." Initially, I titled this book *Excuses in Shackles*, but later, I came up with a more fitting idea. However, the original intent was to hint to the reader that the book is filled with various excuses, some seemingly convincing, others sounding absurd. If an excuse appears convincing, it only shows that many people think that way; it does not mean the excuse is correct, nor does it mean it can convince the one who made it, and vice versa. In other words, regardless of whether people's actions are good or evil, those who act always believe that victory belongs to them. Yet, whether these excuses are convincing or not, the excuse itself objectively exists and is one of the internal motivations driving people's behavior.

Q4: Why is there such an extensive description of thoughts and environments in the novel?

A4: In this novel, I devoted a lot of effort to describing the characters' thoughts and psychological activities, with less direct depiction of their actions and dialogue. I wrote it this way because I believe that the forces that control people's behavior always originate from within. These forces are complex, composed of thinking patterns shaped by the environment, social culture, educational level, political climate, and even the smallest yet most crucial emotions. When inner activity reaches a certain level, it externalizes; all behavior, even inanimate environments, becomes manifestations of the inner self. Humans are creatures capable of lying and disguising their actions, so behavior and language can be false, but the inner self is always the truest. Therefore, in this text, elucidating the characters' inner lives takes precedence.

Q5: Why did you arrange the four parts in this particular order?

A5: The four parts are arranged in the order of "from the imaginary to the real," and "from the micro to the macro." The first part, "The Ripple," depicts the core story for the readers, which is the image of the student's death by falling from a building. The second part, "The Ivory Pendant in the Painting," explains the causes and consequences of the event from the perspective of the school's principal, who started it all. The third part, "Breaking Free," shows why the principal's mistress proposed such a solution. The final part, "A Red Balloon," describes how the matter was resolved from the perspective of an "observer," a policeman. Therefore, the perspective of the first part is particularly microscopic, as a student could hardly understand how many interests and adult thinking styles are involved behind a few photos. The perspectives in the latter three parts gradually expand, revealing the underlying logic with which society deals with certain events, logic deeply rooted in the mindset of a people. No matter the size of the matter, people will use this logic to think and solve problems.

Q6: Why does the novel not have a perfect ending?

A6: I think the word "perfect" in this question should be in quotation marks. What is "perfect"? In most novels, "perfect" means good is rewarded with good, evil is punished with evil, lovers are united, or the protagonist defeats the villain after numerous hardships, as in movies. However, perfect things are not often seen in real life; in fact, they are rare. As I mentioned in the prologue, the author's goal should never be to vent their emotions but to resonate with the reader. If the novel's ending involves punishing the antagonists severely and justice being served, the reader might feel more comfortable, but this kind of treatment only allows readers to vent their emotions and cannot make them empathize because it does not align with reality. Naturally, this would prevent the author from resonating with the reader. If readers realize that the author's words are disconnected from reality, the novel loses its significance in reflecting reality.

Q7: Do such things happen in reality?

A7: Yes, they not only happen, but they have happened, are happening, and will happen in the future. The occurrence of such events depends not only on economic or political circumstances but also on the mindset and behavioral patterns embedded within a group, a nation, or even a culture. This belief is the basis upon which I created this novel. If these events never occurred or will not happen, my writing would have no relevance to reality.

Q8: What is the main theme that this novel intends to convey?

A8: In this novel, I expand upon a specific event, writing about the mental journeys of each key character. Therefore, the novel has multiple themes, most of which involve dissecting the mindset and values of a people. For example, loyalty might be false, but fear is always real. Or when an irrational event occurs, money, power, and sex are often the causes. Overall, I aim to depict, through details, the mental states and thinking patterns of people living today, using the "school" as a relatively microscopic setting to gradually analyze the mental journey of each character, both within the school and society.

Q9: Why are there no specific names mentioned in the novel?

A9: I mentioned in the text that names are meaningless; they are just symbols. What truly matters in reality is each person's role—more specifically, their titles, reputations, and wealth. This is also one of the core ideas that this novel aims to express: in a society driven by interests, a person's power, attractiveness, and money serve as their calling card.

Q10: Does the title of the novel have any special meaning?

A10: "The Living" refers to those who are still

alive. By all logic, they should not experience a funeral. But if people have buried their souls early, then the funeral for the living has already arrived, and only their bodies linger in the world. Death, of course, is a cause for grief, but some will package a sorrowful death as a joyful wedding. However, this wedding is not held for the deceased or for death but to celebrate the union of their soul with filth, giving birth to a new yet evil self.

Q11: Why is there such straightforward depiction of sexual topics in the text?

A11: If you ask me which part of the narrative is the most indispensable, I would say it is the depiction of sex. I mentioned five motivations related to "sex" in the text—for students, sex is an unattainable topic, and love is the purest luxury. For the art teacher, sex is a means of self-protection and a way to gain benefits; for the principal, sex is an emotional outlet; for the police officer's teacher, sex is an embodiment and extension of power; for the police officer himself, sex is an accessory tied to love. As human beings, sex is an instinct engraved in our genes, and many behaviors are driven by sexual desire. The various actions mentioned in the text are no different. Thus, sex is an unavoidable topic in this narrative.

Q12: Is it jarring that the novel is set around a "provincial key high school"?

A12: I do not think so. If the setting were a

"bad" school, it would create even more dissonance. The most straightforward reason is that, in the traditional sense, students in "good schools" are generally more "obedient," giving the impression of being easier to manipulate. Moreover, students in these schools typically come from families with relatively good financial conditions, making it easier for the kinds of crimes described in the novel to emerge. Imagine a school filled with impulsive young people who do not care about consequences; the people in power would probably not dare to act recklessly because money is external, while life is irreplaceable. From elementary to high school, I spent my time in "good schools" and "key classes," so I understand the psychological state of students and teachers growing up in such an environment.

Q13: How much of the plot is based on real events?

A13: The more outrageous the plot, the more likely it is to be real. I consider my imagination lacking and must use real events to fill the gaps in my creativity. If you think a particular scene is unreasonable, it is most likely based on true story.

Annotation

1. (Page 14) "Yuan" (元) is the basic unit of the Chinese currency, similar to the dollar in the United States. It's often referred to as "RMB" (Renminbi), which is the official name of China's currency.

2. (Page 33) "Key high schools" refers to one of the best schools in a city or province. The title of a "key high school" highly depends on the students' performance in the college entrance examination (高考).

3. (Page 46) Some lower-tier brothels in China use pink or purple lighting to attract customers.

4. (Page 60) Sanyu (also known as Chang Yu, or "常玉" in Chinese) was a renowned Chinese-French painter.

5. (Page 63) Zhuge (诸葛) is a famous family in the era of Three Kingdoms (from 220 to 280 AD); Lü Bu (吕布), Ding Yuan (丁原), Dong Zhuo (董卓), and Wang Yun (王允) are all famous people in this era. Wei (魏), Shu (蜀), and Wu (吴) are the names of three kingdoms.

6. (Page 67) The first semester of the school year always starts on the first business day of September in China. Students are required to do homework starting from the first day of primary school. In some cases, even kindergarten

students are assigned homework.

7. (Page 77) Falling in love before entering college (referred to as "young love" or "早恋" in Chinese) is widely considered inappropriate. In most cases, it is punishable in China, even if no sexual activity or physical contact is involved. Sometimes, even an eye contact or a conversation between a boy and a girl could be sufficient grounds for punishment. These punishments may include, but are not limited to, receiving a verbal warning, writing a reflection or apology, being suspended from classes, or being expelled from school. On the contrary, although it is unlawful for principals or teachers to engage in sexual relationships with or to rape underage or adult students, they typically do not face significant punishment or criminal charges (exceptions exist, but they are rare).

8. (Page 78) Dressing in a revealing manner, having a cheek-to-cheek dance with someone of the opposite sex, having romantic or sexual relationships with multiple people (either at the same time or at different times), falling in love with someone without plans for marriage, and engaging in extramarital sex could be punishable by death during certain years (1979–1997) in China. Such acts were classified as the "crime of hooliganism" (流氓罪).

9. (Page 79) "Strike Hard" (abbreviation of "Strike

Hard against Crime Campaign", or "严打" in Chinese) and the "Campaign against Spiritual Pollution" (清除精神污染运动) were both political movements in China.

10. (Page 80) Many people believe that the "Western lifestyle" (e.g., belief in freedom, democracy, and the rule of law) and even Western technological products are tools the United States uses to subvert the government and colonize China. Though it may seem far-fetched to some, this belief is widely held.

11. (Page 89) The term "leader" (领导) typically refers to a government official who holds a higher rank than the speaker.

12. (Page 90) Most jobs in Communist Party or Youth League departments involve "ideological education," which focuses on promoting communism and loyalty to the ruling authorities.

13. (Page 105) The most famous use of the phrase "upholding justice on behalf of heaven" (替天行道) appears in the classic Chinese novel *Water Margin* (《水浒传》). Besides its literal meaning, it symbolically represents "rebellion against the government."

14. (Page 106) The "Cyberspace Affairs Commission" (中央网络安全和信息化委员会办公室，or 网信办) is a department of the

Chinese government. One of its primary tasks is monitoring online speech and taking action against unfavorable content, such as deleting posts, issuing warnings, or notifying law enforcement to make arrests.

15. (Page 116) "Red envelop" (红包), literally meaning "red packet", is a tradition in China. It is either used as gift cash given out during holidays or for special occasions such as weddings or births, or used as a bribe.

16. (Page 123) "Jin Jun Mei" (金骏眉) and "Da Hong Pao" (大红袍) are both types of tea.

17. (Page 130) A score of 145 in math is considered high. In high school, the full scores for Chinese, math, and English exams are 150 points, so 145 points typically means there was only a minor mistake in the exam.

18. (Page 130) Liu Bei is also a famous figure in the era of Three Kingdom. He was the King of Shu. His army was defeated in Yiling (夷陵), leading his death. In the novel *Romance of the Three Kingdoms* (《三国演义》), his death is depicted as a tragedy.

19. (Page 132) Cordyceps is a type of fungus that parasitizes caterpillars and is considered a traditional medicine in China. It is available in some pharmacies.

20. (Page 133) As the victim's family,

representatives, supporters, or lawyers, requesting an explanation or compensation from the school for a student's death could result in being arrested, detained, or charged with crimes, even though such actions are completely reasonable. If these actions embarrass the authorities, they are highly possible to be charged with "picking quarrels and provoking trouble" (寻衅滋事罪), a criminal offense. In a few cases, if the victims or their representatives gain public attention or support, or if they question the government or the authorities, they might be charged with "inciting subversion of state power" (煽动颠覆国家政权罪), which is a much more serious criminal charge.

21. (Page 137) Engaging in prostitution is illegal in China. Such illegal activity could result in job loss.

22. (Page 146) Moving students to the back row is usually considered a form of punishment and humiliation, partly because it makes it harder for students to hear the teacher or see the blackboard clearly. It is also viewed as a signal to others that the student has done something wrong.

23. (Page 156) You can see these kinds of speeches in almost all school-related tragedies or incidents. Generally speaking, the government or authorities do not directly ask students to

make such statements, but students are educated to "protect their alma mater" voluntarily.

24. (Page 189) The term "counter-revolutionary" (反革命) in China has its origins in the early 20th century, particularly during the rise of the Communist movement and later with the founding of the People's Republic of China (PRC). It was primarily used to describe individuals or groups deemed to oppose socialist revolution or the Chinese Communist Party. It is worth noting that although there were legal provisions in China defining the crime of "counter-revolution," the definition was extremely vague. As a result, in judicial practice, the determination of "counter-revolutionary" acts was highly arbitrary. Any behavior or possible thought could be deemed "counter-revolutionary." Specifically, actions such as practicing religion, owning or having previously owned land or businesses, questioning or opposing state policies, protesting against corrupt officials, or having relatives who traveled to Western countries could all be classified as "counter-revolutionary" activities. In the early 1950s alone, over 700,000 people were executed under this charge (some scholars estimate the actual number to be between 1 to 2 million). In 1997, the crime was renamed "inciting subversion of

state power" in the Criminal Law, and in 1999, the term was removed from the Constitution (the term "inciting subversion of state power" is not removed from the Criminal Law).

25. (Page 199) Many schools in China tend to exaggerate grossly their origins and history, often emphasizing a long-standing history. For example, a newly established school might organize a centennial celebration as early as its second year.

26. (Page 200) "Young love" and addiction to Internet (including video games, watching videos online, etc.) are sometimes considered illness in China. So-called "institutions" (sometimes called "training camps", "correction centers", or "schools") for correcting or treating young love, internet addiction and any disobedient behavior are prevalent in some places. The "treatment methods", however, are usually accompanied by violent physical and mental punishment, such as unlawful imprisonment, deprivation of food, beating, electric shock torturing, molestation, sexual abuse, and rape. Those "methods" cause deaths from time to time, but these "institutions" can still be approved by relevant government departments and "legally" exist.

27. (Page 204) Although collective punishment is not supported by Chinese law, family members

(including children, spouse, parents and parents-in-law) of someone who commits a crime may still face repercussions, particularly in political cases. The negative consequences can range from mild to severe, as there are no formal rules governing collective punishment, but such incidents occur frequently.

28. (Page 211) Members of the Chinese Communist Party are not allowed to read the Bible because it is considered a form of cultural invasion or infiltration; for the party members, reading "unauthorized" books, including the Bible, is punishable.